Abigail was lifted.

Why did he seem to be at his worst around her? "Sorry. Answering a text from my mom. Good morning. I just didn't know this was a rideshare."

"Do you want me to get off here?" She leaned in her seat but kept her gaze forward. "I can walk home."

"Don't be ridiculous. I was just surprised." Kingston wanted to add it was good to see her, but she didn't need or want to know that. The dread he had of sharing the ride was gone the minute he realized it was Abigail.

"I guess I should have warned you, but I never say no to a paying customer," Cindy said.

"No problem." He bit back a smile and clicked his seat belt in. "So, what has you using the local taxi, Abigail?" His mood was lighter, and he really wanted to smile. It had nothing to do with her. It didn't.

He was in so much trouble...

A seventh-generation Texan, **Jolene Navarro** fills her life with family, faith and life's beautiful messiness. She knows that as much as the world changes, people stay the same: vow-keepers and heartbreakers. Jolene married a vow-keeper who shows her holding hands never gets old. When not writing, Jolene teaches art to teens and hangs out with her own four almost-grown kids. Find Jolene on Facebook or her blog, jolenenavarro.com.

THE TEXAN'S UNEXPECTED HOME

JOLENE NAVARRO

LOVE INSPIRED
INSPIRATIONAL ROMANCE

ISBN-13: 978-1-335-93727-8

The Texan's Unexpected Home

Recycling programs
for this product may
not exist in your area.

For questions and comments about the quality of this book, please contact us at CustomerService@Harlequin.com.

® is a trademark of Harlequin Enterprises ULC.

Love Inspired
22 Adelaide St. West, 41st Floor
Toronto, Ontario M5H 4E3, Canada
www.LoveInspired.com

Printed in Lithuania

MIX
Paper | Supporting
responsible forestry
FSC® C021394

Cause me to hear thy lovingkindness
in the morning; for in thee do I trust:
cause me to know the way wherein I should walk;
for I lift up my soul unto thee.
—*Psalm* 143:8

To Jesus Alfredo Navarro "Fred."
You are my home. Thank you for encouraging me
for the last thirty-eight years. I think I might
finally be figuring this thing out.

Chapter One

The heavy humidity settled on Kingston Zayas's shoulders as he stepped out of the San Antonio airport. With a sigh, he called Axel Mendoza—his best friend and new business partner. If this plan derailed, they would be standing in the wreckage of their dream. He couldn't let down the one person who'd always had his back.

"Hey, Kingston." Axel's always-serious voice sounded more melancholy than usual. "Are you in Rio Bella? Had a chance to talk to your mom?"

"No. The flight was delayed. I'm just now in San Antonio and trying to find a ride. Did you know it's over two hours from here? It's really in the middle of nowhere."

"Before you told me about your ranch, I'd never heard of the town."

"It's not my ranch." He closed his eyes. According to his uncle Juan Carlos Zayas's will, at least one-third of it was technically his. He still didn't understand why.

"I just want to see how our boys are doing. Did they get settled in at Hawthorn stables?"

"Everyone but Fuego. The barn fire was too much for him. They had to tranq him to doctor the wounds. Physically, he'll recover, but I don't see him finishing his scheduled races this season. We've turned him out to pasture for now."

"They counted him out before, and he was proving them wrong. I'm not giving up on him. I'll talk to my mother and cousin about boarding him on the ranch. With some one-on-one time, I can get him on the track for next season." He scanned the area. "I need to hang up if I'm going to find a way to Rio Bella."

"Sir?" An older woman with two steel-gray braids approached him.

Disconnecting the call, he stepped back and narrowed his eyes at the woman. She seemed harmless enough, but one could never really tell.

"I'm sorry to interrupt, but I heard you say you're heading to Rio Bella?"

He nodded, slowly, not sure where this was going.

She pointed to a two-tone burnt orange Suburban. *Rio Bella Delivery* was written in bold cursive on the door. He couldn't imagine it coming out of the factory in those colors, even in the 1990s, if he'd guessed the decade right. They didn't make them that big anymore. It was a tank. Four people were inside, looking at him.

"Are you a wedding guest at the Tres Amigos Ranch and Resort? Letti and Naomi hired me to pick everyone up."

This woman knew his mother and cousin. Naomi was Juan Carlos's oldest child, and the only one who inherited the ranch along with Kingston and his mother, Letti. The rest of the family was not happy.

"Oh, sorry. I'm Cindy French." She held out her hand. "I usually don't accost strangers at the airport, but I heard you needed a way to Rio Bella and thought you might be a weddin' guest. If not, sorry. I'll leave you to it."

"No." Words. He needed words. His poor brain was trashed after getting the horses out of the fire, finding a safe place to stall them and then dealing with the insurance. "I mean, yes. I need a ride to the ranch, but I'm not a wedding guest." He really didn't want to be telling his business to people. Hopefully, she would just let him go along. "I'll pay you."

Her smile returned with a vengeance. "Oh, never mind that, sweetheart. I was paid to pick people up at the airport and take them to the ranch. You, sir, are a person that fits that description. Is that the only bag you have?" Her brows were raised in disbelief.

He looked down at his secondhand duffel bag. It was everything he owned. His whole life had been lost in the fire. It was unreal that just forty-eight hours ago, he had come home from an event to see flames in the tack room window. Their apartment was above the stables, but his only concern had been to get the horses out.

"Are you okay?" Her head was tilted, and he found real concern in the light green eyes.

"Yeah. Sorry. Just stuck in some thoughts. Yes, this is my only bag."

She reached for it and slung it over her shoulder. "Well, come on. We got to hit the road. You working at the ranch?"

"That's the plan." If he kept his answers short, she should get the hint that he didn't want to talk.

Getting the third-row seat was not conducive for a six-foot-four frame. His height had always caused him problems. At sixteen, he'd had to give up his dream of being a jockey. And he couldn't count how many times people had asked him about playing football or basketball.

Cindy introduced him to the other passengers. After that, he rested his head and closed his eyes. He was functioning on about two hours of sleep.

The Suburban stopped moving and he sat up and blinked a couple times. He didn't even remember falling asleep.

Getting out of the car was worse than climbing in. He yawned and stretched his tight muscles. Between the plane and the car trip, his knees were stiff and his body was tired.

Pulling his sunglasses out of his jacket pocket, he took a deep breath. Well, he was here. He didn't remember ever visiting his uncle's Hill Country ranch. Juan Carlos Zayas had been loud with an overpowering presence. As a child, he had been terrified of him.

To say Kingston wasn't close to his family would be an understatement. His mother, Letti, was much younger than Juan Carlos, and his only family. In Kingston's memories, she had avoided her brother as much as possible, with good reason. One mistake or bad choice would have his uncle on a rampage for hours.

As an adult, he understood his mother's need to relocate so many times. Any new boyfriend or shiny opportunity to start over, they moved. It would fail and they'd end up back in Juan Carlos's home in Dallas. He would yell, telling her how she was in this mess because she hadn't listened.

It had been on one of those returns to Dallas that Kingston had met Axel.

A week after he turned thirteen, there had been another big fight. This time, his uncle demanded Kingston stay with him and finish school. Letti left for California, and Kingston stayed over with Axel's family as much as possible. Axel's dad trained racehorses, and Kingston found his passion.

His family had all gone their separate ways long ago. But now he needed their help if there was any chance of saving the dream he and his best friend had put everything into.

With a sigh, Kingston scanned the area. There was a Spanish-style hacienda that looked to be under major renovations to his right, and a path that went to the left.

Branches of ancient live oak trees twisted and sprawled over the path, casting deep shadows. For a moment he stood still. It was more beautiful than he'd expected.

Why had he inherited the ranch along with his mother and oldest cousin? Juan Carlos had two other children from a second marriage. Why Kingston and not them?

A smiling teen pulled up in a bright green four-wheel utility vehicle. She had room for four, so she took the wedding guests to their cabins.

"Can't believe this is all you have." Cindy eyed him curiously as she handed him the duffel bag. "Naomi told me they were short-staffed."

Growing up, Kingston had learned to be good at small talk and putting people at ease, but today his brain was not firing on all cylinders.

He tried to remember the last time he'd seen Naomi. She had always been kind, but standoffish. Avoiding the family as much as possible was a trait she shared with Letti and Kingston.

Letti and Naomi had joined forces after Juan Carlos's death and had been trying to get Kingston to the ranch for a few months now. With the race season starting, it had been easy to ignore them. Hopefully, they wouldn't hold that against him when he asked for help.

"The office is down that way." Cindy's gravelly voice brought him back to the present as she pointed to the path before returning to the rear of her vehicle to pop the trunk.

He lifted his bag over his shoulder and turned to the path. He had planned on ignoring the stipulation in his uncle's will that he had to live on the ranch for a year. He didn't have that kind of time to spend away from his racehorses. Plus, there was no way his mother would be able to stay in one place for more than six months either. Especially Rio Bella.

From the stories he'd heard, this place and the people who lived here had broken her heart.

But now Kingston needed Letti and Naomi to agree to let him use his share of the ranch as collateral to rebuild his barn in North Texas.

"Cindy!" A woman came running at them from the path on his left. A flowing black skirt flew around her as she raced past, pulling a red canvas wagon behind her. Probably a warning flag.

Her turquoise-rimmed glasses were a cat-eye cut and sat a little crooked across her nose. "I'm so glad you're here," she gasped, nearly out of breath.

She hugged the woman as if she was her long-lost mother. No one had ever greeted him with that much enthusiasm.

Her raven-black hair danced around her face and over her shoulders. Remains of a deconstructed braid proved it had been fixed at one point this morning. He smiled. Now the rebellious curls refused to be tamed. The ends were lighter and a bit frayed, as if she had spent countless hours in the sun and not so much in a salon.

His driver hugged her tight, then stepped back. "Oh, sweetheart. I'm sorry I'm late. The Westens' plane had been delayed. But I found this poor gentleman at the airport. He was looking for a ride to the ranch." Cindy fluttered her hand at him, then leaned forward into the back of her Suburban for a wooden crate.

"Oh, so rude of me. Hi. I'm Abigail Harris." She wiped her hand on her skirt then held it out to him with a smile that lit up her whole face. "Are you here for the wedding?"

"Nope," Cindy answered before he could say anything.

"He doesn't talk much, but he said he was here for work."
She squinted at him. "I think."

For a moment, Abigail's eyes flared with excitement,
then quickly narrowed in confusion. They were an interesting gray-green color, attractively framed by those bright
turquoise glasses. She glanced down then up. He got the
impression she wasn't impressed. That hurt the pride a bit.

"You're the new wrangler?" she asked, clearly not believing it.

He wasn't sure what job a wrangler did. Wasn't that
some sort of cowboy? He was pretty sure it wasn't him. "I
don't think so?"

Both women laughed as Abigail nodded. "Never seen a
wrangler in such fancy shoes. Welcome to the Tres Amigos. I'm the event coordinator. Tonight, we're hosting our
first wedding." She took the crate from Cindy and carefully
placed it in her wagon.

"Can I help?" he asked.

"It's just these four boxes." She took another and placed
it with the others. "They're custom handblown glasses for
the wedding party. Staggers my mind how much they cost."
Once all four were stacked, she turned the wagon around.
"I know you just got here, but we're short-staffed and could
use an extra pair of hands. Naomi and Letti are with the
family so they're not available. You're staying in the bunkhouse, right? Follow me, then you'll turn right. You can put
your stuff away and come over to the event barn. You'll
see the huge white tents between that barn and the stables."

Energy still swirled around her as she pulled the full
wagon away. He just stood there, watching her go. A million words had come from her lips, and he was still pro-
cessing them. Her leather boots had turquoise threading

that matched the threading on her black shirt, skirt and glasses. She looked very Texas.

Cindy cleared her throat, her hand out. Kingston had forgotten her. *Bad manners.* He pulled out his wallet.

"Oh, no. Naomi has me on retainer for the ranch. I just wanted to give you this." She waved off his money and he saw the card in her hand. "If you want to go anywhere, just give me a call. There aren't no cabs or any of those fancy rideshare apps out here like all the city folks use. I know all the written and unwritten history around these parts. We've got some great food you won't taste anywhere else. I have a list of all the best sights, and some places not so good but lots of fun." She laughed as if she'd made a joke. "There's a couple of stores in town where you can get a pair of good working boots."

He glanced down at his footwear while she was talking. They were the dress shoes he had been wearing the night the fire destroyed his life's work.

"Welcome to Rio Bella. Population 415. Just give me a call if you need anything. I make deliveries too."

They stood there just looking at each other and for a moment he feared she was going to hug him. Instead, she gave him little pat on his shoulder and disappeared into her tank of a vehicle.

His stomach had been in knots since he'd spotted those flames. Now he had to convince two women he hadn't seen in a while to help him rebuild his dream. This second half of the racing season might be a wash. But if he and Axel could be up and running by the end of summer, they could hit next season strong.

First step. "To the bunkhouse then scope out the wedding." He needed to find his mother and cousin, but he could do that later. "Coward." The ancient trees nodded in agreement.

* * *

The ceremony had started on time, and everything was finally in place for the reception. Abigail had just spoken with the caterers to make sure all was set. Her heart had almost returned to normal but not quite yet. So much could still go wrong.

She glanced at her watch then took her phone out and checked for any emergency messages. Jacob, the seasoned ranch maintenance person, had texted that his cleanup crew had called in sick. His crew was made up of two local high school boys who had already complained about working Saturday night.

She groaned inwardly. So, it would be just her and Jacob on cleanup.

She opened the camera on her phone and glanced at her hair. Yes, it was still in place since she'd redone it. When she had gone into the restroom earlier, a horrified gasp had flown from her lungs. She'd been a sweaty mess who looked as if she'd tangled with a tornado and lost. Could she have looked any worse to meet the new hire?

The tall, put-together newest employee must have wondered how such a mess of a woman could be trusted to organize important events. No wonder his stare had burned into her with a raw intensity.

She had been in such a rush and so flustered by his presence she had forgotten to get his name. She couldn't imagine what job Naomi had hired him for.

He looked like he belonged on a ranch as much as she belonged in a five-star hotel.

Spoiler, she didn't. Not for a minute. But his hair was immaculately tousled in just the right places, and he had a five-o'clock shadow that called attention to a perfect jawline that… She shook her head.

Nope. Not wasting silly thoughts on a man's face. He probably hadn't been impressed by her at all.

With her free hand, she smoothed down the few unruly strands that fought at being restrained. She had tried to go for a loose, romantic braid, but that hadn't worked at all. Now the top was pulled in a clip and the rest hung around her shoulders. Her makeup was freshly applied.

There was movement to her left. *Please don't let some wild animal or feral cat destroy the runners and center-pieces.* Careful not to startle whatever it was, she eased around the end of the table.

"Roar!" Leo, her six-year-old son, jumped up. He waved his arms over his head. "I'm a dinosaur, Momma. Did I scare you?"

Her hand over her heart, she took a few deep breaths. "Leo, what are you doing out here? Tio Joaquin is going to pick you up at the office." The head housekeeper had volunteered to watch Leo until her brother could get here. Of all the days for the babysitter to get sick.

With a pout, he crossed his arms. Her little boy was the spitting image of her grandfather. "He called and said there was an emergency with his cows, and Gloria was too busy to play. I want to be with you."

"I know, sweetheart, but remember we have the next two days together. Tonight, I have to work. Go to the office, okay?" She was going to have a talk with Joaquin. He could have called one of her other brothers or their grandfather to get Leo. Now she would have to use time she didn't have to straighten this out.

"I want to stay with you." Leo ducked down and went under the table.

"Leo, come out." She dialed her oldest brother, Cyrus. No answer. "I'm counting. Five. Four." Next, she called

Lucas. "Three." It went to voicemail. Joaquin's phone did the same. She had lost track of her countdown. "Great. Leo, I need you to go to the office now."

"Nope. I'm a dinosaur in a cave. You're a dinosaur hunter. Come get me."

Normally, she loved her son's imagination, but not right now. The wedding ceremony would be over in fifteen minutes and the guests would be coming this way. She dropped down and lifted the edge of the tablecloth. Leo sat cross-legged at the far end, all smiles.

"Isn't this cool?"

"Right now, I'm upset because you're not listening."

Someone cleared their throat from above her. Eyes closed, she asked God to help her remain calm. She needed His strength and wisdom, because she was running on empty.

As she backed out, she bumped her head on the edge of the table. Her clip snapped and her hair fell around her face. "No. No. No." She searched for the little black hair accessory and her glasses fell off.

"Do you need help?" The deep, smooth voice was from earlier today. The new employee was about to see her as a total mess again. So that answered the question from earlier. Yes, it could be worse.

With a deep breath, she backed all the way out and stood.

She smiled and tried to smooth her hair. Her glasses were at her feet. When she went to pick them up, she collided with him trying to do the same. "Ouch. I'm sorry." She stood, smoothing out her outfit. Great, she even had grass on her skirt.

He handed her the glasses. "Sorry. I was just trying to help." Tilting his head, he glanced behind her. "Is there a problem?"

"A small one." She would not cry. Control, she had control of her emotions. Putting her glasses in place, she found his intense gaze focused on her.

"Is there something I can do to help?" His tentative expression made his thoughts clear. She was beyond help. He was probably right.

Her pride was on the ground, way past any heroic CPR efforts, so she tilted her head and smiled. "Are you already on the clock, Mr....?"

"Just Kingston. You needed all hands on deck so I'm here to do whatever you need."

"Momma!" Leo was standing now.

She reached over and grabbed his hand before he could dive under the table again. This was her first big event for the resort, and she had to prove she was worth the salary and benefits *before* she told them she was a DeLeon by birth. "This is Leo, my son. He's supposed to be at the office waiting to be picked up." She pointed to the limestone house on the other side of an old wooden barn.

He stiffened a little, then looked at Leo as if he had never seen a child before. "You just need me to walk him to the house over there and someone will take him?"

"Yes. Gloria Hernandez. She's the head housekeeper. Leo, be a good helper and show Mr. Kingston the office. Will you introduce him to Ms. Gloria?"

"Okay. When you get home, you'll come say good-night?"

"I promise. In the morning we'll make dino pancakes." She leaned down and hugged him closely. She was doing this for him, so they could have a better life. But it still hurt when she wasn't the one to tuck him in. "I love you."

"Love you too, Momma." He smiled up at Mr. Kingston and took his hand. "I'll show you where the office is, and you can meet Ms. Gloria. She makes the best brownies."

The tall man who had stood as if he owned the world

earlier now looked a bit lost. He glanced at her one last time before allowing her son to drag him along as he chatted about Ms. Gloria and all her special treats.

Who was this man? Voices came up from the slope that led to the wedding platform. The guests were coming. She dusted off her skirt and took the hair band off her wrist to tie a neat knot at the base of her neck. At least, she hoped it was neat.

All thoughts of Mr. Kingston had to be pushed aside. This wedding had to be a success.

Chapter Two

Leo's small, fragile hand took his and led the way with total confidence. Kingston forced the muscles in his hand to relax. Wouldn't do to break the poor tyke's fingers.

If he'd been smart, he would have stayed in the old limestone bunkhouse, waiting for the morning to venture out.

But no. He had to volunteer. One minute he's running into a burning barn, next he's holding hands with a small child. His brain hurt from the whiplash. Served him right. He had been too fascinated by the event coordinator, and he didn't have time for that.

Then the word *Momma* became attached to her. That meant she was either married or a single mom. Neither of those options were in his playbook. Kids needed stability. Memories of his unstable childhood flooded his mind. Single mothers deserved long-term commitments and that wasn't him.

"You're new here?" The little guy carried on a conversation without knowing the whirlwind in Kingston's mind. "So, you're not related to us?"

That made him pause. What was the kid talking about? "I'm from Dallas."

"Is that a longer drive than San Antonio?"

"Yes. I flew to San Antonio, then drove over two hours to get here." Did all kids ask these kinds of questions?

"Okay." He nodded as if that answered a very important question. "So, you're from far away. That's good. You're not our cousin or something, right?" The boy waved to people as they passed the barn. Smiling, they waved back.

This short walk was becoming very long. Kingston looked over his shoulder. Abigail was guiding people to long tables covered in cleverly arranged fruit and appetizers.

"Um, cousin?" What were they talking about now? He was having a hard time focusing.

Leo nodded with the seriousness of a judge. "Tito says Momma needs a husband. But Tio Cyrus said the town is too small. All the good ones are either married or related to us. I think Tito would like it if you ask Momma out on a date."

His feet stopped moving. Abigail *was* a single mother. On the hunt for a husband? Looking down at the dark-haired boy, he just blinked. Leo looked at him with pure innocence.

Don't overreact, he's just a kid. He doesn't know what he's talking about. Just keep walking. The faster they got to the woman named Gloria, the faster he could hide in the bunkhouse. The best way to derail this conversation was by not responding.

Leo didn't like silence.

"Are you working on Tres Amigos Ranch? Are you a cowboy? I come from a long line of cowboys. I'm going to be the best cowboy around, like my Tio Lucas. He's a champion. But Tito says rodeo tricks aren't real cowboy work. He says Tio Joaquin is the best cowboy. But he never leaves the ranch. I like people, so I want to be a rodeo cowboy like Tio Lucas. But to make Tito happy I'll work on the ranch also."

How many uncles did this kid have? *Don't engage. It will only encourage him. Don't do it.* "Your grandfather?" Ugh. He did it.

"Well, really my great-grandfather. I never met my grandfather. He died with my grandmother and my great-grandmother and a great uncle in a car crash when Momma was a little kid like me. Tito Lucas was in the car too. He's the only one that didn't die. But no one really talks about it. My dad moved to California. I think he forgot about me. Tio Cyrus says good riddance. Are you a cowboy? You don't look like a cowboy." Leo eyed his shoes.

Kingson's heart went out to the spunky little guy. He knew what it was like to be forgotten.

They finally made it to the office. Kingston blew out a puff of air in relief. "Looks like we're here. We just need to find Gloria." She would take responsibility for the kid.

Leo bounded up the steps and went through the door. "Gloria, I'm back." He yelled as if he had just made her day. "I have Mr. Kingston with me."

Kingston couldn't stop smiling. The kid's father might have left his son behind, but apparently Leo didn't feel alone or unloved.

He stepped into the limestone house that had to be at least one hundred years old, give or take a decade. Shiny hardwood floors connected all the rooms. To the right was a sitting area with clapboard walls and soft blue, pink and yellow accents. Over the rocked fireplace hung a large portrait of Naomi's mother, the one true love of Juan Carlos's life. Whenever his uncle hadn't been lecturing him, he had been telling stories about her. She had brought out a different side of him, a side her loss had chiseled away. There had been a family picture too. He looked around.

It hung on the wall behind him. Naomi as a toddler on

Juan Carlos's lap. Naomi's mother at his right shoulder. His mother, Letti, at his left.

There was a twenty-year difference between the siblings. His mom had been too young to remember her parents. Juan Carlos had come to the States to raise her. His uncle never missed an opportunity to talk about family pride and their Cuban roots deep in the rich soil of his homeland. He studied the picture. Even then his mom looked sad. His uncle looked as stern as ever, even surrounded by the family he claimed to love. The fact that there were no pictures or portraits of his second wife or other two children seemed wrong. Probably one reason the marriage didn't last.

Needing to change his thoughts, Kingston looked to the left. What was probably a parlor at one time now served as a very feminine office in the same colors as the front room. Leo had disappeared through an archway.

Following him, he stepped into a very modern farm kitchen. From here, he could hear a washer and dryer running somewhere in the hallway. The smell of baked goods was stronger here. An assortment of sweets covered a highly polished butcher-block island.

Leo had his mouth full. "These are the best."

Kingston glanced around. "Do you know where Gloria is?"

The boy shook his head. "Maybe the laundry room," he mumbled around a mouthful of brownie.

The back door opened and slammed. A small but solid-built woman wearing a black apron over jeans, boots and a white shirt rushed from the hallway. She had a name tag that said Gloria.

Her arms were wrapped around a large basket of white sheets, some of which were falling over the rim.

"Mr. Leo. Did you run off to see your mom? *Te dije que-*

date aquí. I turn my back for a minute, and he runs off."
She eyed Kingston. "And who is your new friend?"

"This is Mr. Kingston. Momma made him bring me.
I'm sorry I didn't stay like you told me to." The boy barely
looked contrite before smiling again. "He's a new ranch
hand. But I don't think he's a cowboy."

He held out his hand. "I'm Kingston. My first task was
to deliver Leo to you."

With a tight smile, she nodded at him, then backed away
with one hand on the boy's arm.

"No cause ninun problema," she whispered through gritted teeth as she tried to maintain her smile. *"Tengo que
trabajar."*

"He wasn't a problem."

She stiffened and stood straight. "Oh. You speak Spanish."

"Nothing to be sorry about."

With a tentative nod, she looked at the clock above the
stove. "His cousin, Emma, might be the one to pick him up.
One of the cabins needs clean sheets. I'm afraid we can't
trust him to stay put." She looked at the boy with affection
and attempted to put a few wild curls in place.

"I love Emma." The little boy jumped around "She's so
much fun. A lot more fun than her dad, Tío Cyrus."

Gloria turned to him. "I'm sorry to ask, but—"

"Don't worry. I've got him." Did he just volunteer to
spend more time with a child? "We've got things to discuss. Right, Leo?"

"Yes!"

She hurried away. They stared at each other. Now what
was he supposed to do?

Leo grabbed his hand and led him to the bar stools.
"Let's get milk and we can talk about cowboys, why boots
are important, horses and taking my mom on a date."

The kid didn't let things go, did he? "I'll get the milk. I lost my boots in a fire. I can talk horses all day and night. I have thoroughbreds. Racehorses. Let's pull the reins on dating your mom. You don't know me and shouldn't set your mom up with strangers."

A stranger who'd be leaving soon and refused to be the kind of man who leaves a kid who counts on him. He checked his phone. When was Emma getting here?

Abigail's face hurt from smiling. The last of the guests had gone to their cabins. Cindy had driven the others to their lodgings in town after the wedding couple had made a spectacular exit in a helicopter.

Apparently, she had not made sure the landing pad was far enough away. The guests had been out of range, but some of the tables had not and there was wedding propaganda scattered across the pasture. At least everyone had laughed, loving it.

Naomi and Letti had left with the groom's parents, who were close family friends. It was hard to tell how the two women felt about the event. Was it enough to overcome her being a DeLeon?

She checked her phone. No reply from any of her brothers or grandfather.

Judge Rubio would surely be sympathetic if she strangled them. Not once since coming home had she asked them to watch Leo. They were busy, but this had been an emergency and her first big event in her new job.

Had it been on purpose? They had adamantly protested her taking the job on the Tres Amigos Ranch and Resort. Now that the Zayas family was back on the ranch, her grandfather claimed her working here drove his blood pressure up.

Abhorrence might be too tame a word to describe how her family felt about this place. But her son's needs trumped any family feud. Juan Carols Zayas was dead. Her grandfather needed to let it go. Tres Amigos was the only option in the area where she could do what she was trained for, and no one else was going to offer her this kind of salary and benefits.

"Are you sure you want to stay and help? Not part of your job." Jacob held a roll of plastic trash bags in his gloved hand.

She took the roll and pulled a couple of bags off it. "My job is to make sure the event runs smoothly from beginning to end. It's not over until the evidence of two hundred people eating and dancing here is gone." She was talking to herself. Jacob had left.

Gloves on, she walked to the outskirts of the reception area to pick-up debris the helicopter had scattered.

"You organize, plan, run and clean up for all the events? I hope they pay well." The new ranch hand, Mr. Tall and Intense, leaned against a tent pole. The white gauzy material danced behind him in the night breeze.

It was well after midnight, and Kingston looked as if he had just stepped into a photo shoot. All he needed to make the picture complete was to pull on his cuff link, lower his chin and look at her through his thick lashes. He was unreal. But it would look good on their webpage.

Abigail didn't need a mirror to know her own look was swept by a tornado. "Our cleaning crew called in sick. I wasn't going to leave Jacob to do it alone. Thank you for taking Leo." She handed Kingston one of the bags. "Here. You can take the tables. Gloves are over there. When the trash is picked up, then start putting the table runners in the marked boxes. The candles and candlesticks have boxes

too. The caterers took care of the food and service ware."
One thing at least that she didn't have to worry about. She
might get home before the sunrise.

He blinked a couple of times like he didn't understand.
He turned his gaze to the farm tables under the tent and
studied them for a minute.

"Is there a problem?" Maybe she'd overstepped. He
wasn't on the ranch for this sort of job. But they had a
small staff and helping each other seemed the right thing
to do. "I'm sorry if—"

"No. I'm good. I was just wondering what we're going to
do with all the fresh flowers. Seems a waste to just throw
them in the trash."

With a sigh, she looked at all the greenery and flowers.
"I arranged for the centerpieces to be donated to our local
churches. Cindy will deliver them in the morning. But I
hadn't thought about the ones that can't be reused."

"That seems like such a waste. Here." He handed her a
bundle. "You should take some home."

Her heart fluttered for a minute. When was the last time
someone gave her flowers? "I...um. Thank you." She took
the flowers and fought the urge to pull them close and inhale. "I'll take these. You know we could put the rest in the
compost. They'll feed the earth."

"Good idea." He went to work.

She tried to keep her focus on the task in front of her
and not where Mr. Kingston was working. She tried and
failed. Finally, they finished loading the garbage and met
in the middle of the tent.

"It's time to get the ranch truck so we can load all these
bags. Do you want to go get it or should I?" Abigail said.

He grinned. "Since I have no clue where it would be,
maybe you should do that."

"Right." She walked backward. "You wouldn't know where to go." She bumped into something and stumbled. Mr. Kingston reached for her and placed his hands on her upper arms.

They were warm and gentle. Strange for such a—

"Are you okay? Do you need me to go with you?" He stepped back as quickly as he had moved to her side.

She was a little dizzy. Was it because of him? Her stomach rumbled—more like yelled in protest. Horrified, she looked down. Maybe it wasn't as loud as she feared. She could hope.

"You didn't eat dinner?"

He'd heard it. "No."

"When was the last time you ate?"

"It was…" She stopped to think. Surely she ate at one point today.

"I'm going to take that confused look on your face as a long time ago."

"This is embarrassing." No wonder she'd been having dizzy spells the last hour or so. It wasn't a reaction to Mr. Kingston after all. That was a relief. "My brothers are going to kill me for not taking care of myself. They already hate that I work here for the enemy."

"The enemy?"

"Don't tell anyone, but I'm a DeLeon. The women who own this ranch are from the Zayas family." With a stage whisper, she leaned closer. "Sworn mortal enemies. The older woman, Letti, I heard secretly married my uncle Diego. When he was killed in a car crash, she inherited his part of our ranch land. Or somehow Juan Carlos stole it from him to make his ranch bigger. Depends on who you talk to."

She sighed. "The Zayases are the reason my grandfather lost his whole family. I'm not clear on the details. But that's what my grandfather yells about anyway. The Zayas family left and refused to give the land back. The families hate each other." Her hand flew to her mouth to stop more words from coming out. She had read somewhere that lack of sleep had the same effect on the body as drinking too much. She had never done that, but what other reason would she have for spewing that family gossip all over him? "Sorry. I don't know Letti and Naomi's side of the story. Forget I said anything. It happened three decades ago. I want Letti and Naomi to depend on me before they find out I'm a DeLeon. I can't afford to lose this job."

She waved her hand around, hoping to wipe away her words. "Please don't repeat anything I've said. I really like Letti and Naomi. They've been great to work for. I'll tell them soon. I'm just not ready yet."

He grinned at her. "Your secrets are safe with me. Come on. Let's go to the office."

"The office?" She hesitated. The site wasn't clear. There were still things she needed to do before she could leave.

"I saw barbecue and sides wrapped up and put in the refrigerator." He leaned closer and whispered, "While I was hanging out with Leo, the groom's mom said the staff could have the leftovers. We've cleaned this area. Just need to move the boxes and load up the greenery in the truck. That can happen tomorrow. I haven't eaten either."

"I'm not leaving till the whole area is cleaned up," she protested.

Kingston shook his head. "Now you're just being stubborn. I'll grab this last load of trash, throw it in the truck, and then we go get something to eat."

The café lights were strung in a zigzag over them. Earlier tonight, the tent had been a portal to a fairy-tale garden. She looked around. Now it had an abandoned, neglected vibe.

An owl screeched in the darkness, past the tent area.

Kingston stopped mid-toss. "What was that? I hadn't expected the place to be so…so wild."

"That was an owl." Coming up next to him, she topped off the pile of abandoned decorations with the last armful of vines. "This isn't wild. We are surrounded by thousands of acres of untamed land, but right here? No, this is pretty domesticated. Where did you come from?"

"Dallas. The wedding seemed very successful."

That was a swift change of topic. "I hope so. Which of my brothers picked up Leo?" The big ranch truck was rattling their way. Jacob was returning.

"Your niece, Emma. Leo was very excited about that."

She chuckled. "Yes. He loves her. I'm glad someone in my family showed up."

"She said a pen of young bulls got out and broke into a pasture full of cows. All-hands-on-deck situation apparently. Your brothers called Emma to pick up Leo. She apologized for being late."

Oh. "Then it was a real emergency and wasn't on purpose."

"Letting the bulls out?" He sounded confused.

"No. Not picking up Leo." She had told them not to interrupt her today and they had taken care of everything without contacting her.

"Why would they do that on purpose?" He turned after throwing his last load on the pile. He was closer than she expected. He took a quick step back, took off the gloves, then stuffed them in his pockets. She crossed her arms over her chest.

Jacob pulled up next to the tent then came around the ranch truck and lowered the tailgate. "Hop on, I'll give you a ride to the office. I've got stuff in the cab. You'll have to sit here. We'll eat, then call it a night. You've been running around here since seven a.m." He went to the front and waited for them to sit before pulling onto the drive.

"You didn't answer my question," Kingston said.

She blinked. "Sorry, my brain is a bit foggy. What did you ask?"

"Why would they leave Leo here after you made arrangements for them to pick him up?"

"Oh. That's me being paranoid because, you know, the whole family feud thing. Thought maybe they were trying to get me fired." Her tummy rumbled again. It had no manners. She studied her feet as the road moved under them. The new hire hadn't complained once, despite not looking the part of a ranch hand. "What were you doing in Dallas?"

"Oh, um. I work with racehorses." Now he seemed uneasy.

She frowned. That was a whole different world than a working ranch and venue resort. Why was he here?

Chapter Three

❧

The truck stopped in front of the office and Kingston jumped down. His feet didn't like the impact. Yeah, he would get some boots as soon as he could get into town. Turning, he held his hand out to Abigail.

Did his mother and cousin expect all their employees to work twenty-hour days? And Abigail suspected her brothers of sabotage? What had he walked into here?

"Kingston, is that you? When did you get here? You said you'd never…" Naomi raced down the steps. "Abigail? Goodness. What are you still doing here? It's two in the morning." Her gaze darted between Kingston and Abigail.

Jacob came around the front of the truck. "Ms. Zayas. My cleaning crew called in sick, and she and Mr. Kingston stayed to help."

"We're almost finished." Abigail started. "I can go—"

"No." Kingston moved closer to her. "You're eating before you do anything else." He needed to get his thoughts together before his cousin and mother hit him with a thousand questions.

"You haven't eaten?" Naomi's confusion turned to concern.

"It's been busy and with the lack of staff, she hasn't eaten all day. So, after we gathered the trash and greenery, I told her to come get some of the leftover barbecue."

"Of course." Naomi came down the steps and put a hand on Abigail's shoulder. "I never meant for you to stay this long. Or to go without eating. I'm sorry I didn't check on you. It's been a day, and it just keeps going. There's plenty to eat and then you're going home. Letti and I can take care of the rest in the morning."

The door creaked open. They all turned to the loud gasp. "Kingston!" His mother bounded down the steps and flew at him. Her chestnut hair had streaks of silver. She was tall and solid. He staggered, but wrapped his arms around her and balanced them.

"Hey, Mom." Her arms gripped him tighter as if she was afraid he would leave. She had never greeted him like this. He wasn't sure how to handle it.

"You came. You said you couldn't, but you're here." Her words muffled against his shoulder. Leaning back, she cupped his face. "Look at you. Kingston Juan Carlos Zayas! You've been ignoring my calls. Now you show up at two in the morning and just…" She tapped his face in a mock slap. "I'm upset with you."

And this was one of the many reasons he had stayed away. She would play the victim and make him feel guilty for not being a devoted son. Never mind she was the one who'd left him first.

It was too complicated to unravel, and he was tired. His brain was total mush. He glanced at Naomi, and as usual, she hung back, her fingers interlocked. Concern was stamped all over her features, but her focus was now on him and his mother.

"Wait." A deep frown wrinkled Abigail's forehead. "Zayas? I thought your name was Kingston."

"It is, but..." The need to apologize seized him even though he hadn't lied.

"Oh, Abigail, this is Kingston Zayas, my son and the third owner of the ranch." Letti looked up at him with complete adoration.

He shifted uncomfortably as Abigail went pale.

"He's finally here." Letti's dark eyes watered. "Where you belong. The three of us are here on the ranch together."

He shook his head. This wasn't his home. He'd watched that go up in flames. He lifted his gaze to Naomi. She was chewing on her bottom lip and had her arms wrapped around her waist. She didn't seem to share his mother's overly dramatic sentiment.

Abigail took a deep breath. "You're one of the owners and I've been..." She blinked a couple of times.

While he had been focused on his mother and cousin, Abigail had started slipping away.

He wanted to reach for her and tell her not to worry about anything she had said or done while they were working together. She had been so relaxed, not worried about impressing him. He had been just another ranch hand.

"I have to go. It's so late." She was halfway to the side of the house, where he assumed she had her car.

"You can't drive without getting some food in your system," he called after her, resisting the urge to give chase.

"I'll eat when I get home."

"A dizzy spell while driving is not good." He was at the door. "Let me make a plate for you." He fought to keep the bizarre desperation out of his voice. He wanted her to smile at him again. "Just stand there a minute and I'll gather up some food for you to take."

Kingston didn't wait for her to answer. He ran into the kitchen and pulled a couple to-go boxes from the cabinet and the large aluminum pans from the commercial refrigerator. Finding a bag took longer than expected.

His heart raced at the thought of her leaving before he returned outside. He went to the cabinet and dug for a container to put a few brownies in.

Not seeing him, Jacob bumped into the cabinet door. "Sorry, sir."

The old cowboy's posture was stiffer than before he had heard Kingston's last name.

Was it weird that he preferred them thinking he was just another ranch hand? "Just Kingston. And I was the one under the counter, so no apologies needed."

Taking a deep breath, he looked Jacob in the eye. He hated that they thought he had lied to them like some undercover cop. "Sorry about the misunderstanding. I never meant to fool anyone. You both worked hard and I'm glad I could help. Are we good?"

He held out his hand and waited. Some of the weight he carried slid off as the old cowboy took it and they shook. He suspected it wouldn't go quite that smoothly with Abigail—if she even waited for him to explain.

Abigail tried to smile, but she was too nervous. She had told Kingston about her name and the hostility between their families. She'd thought it wouldn't matter to the new guy.

But he was a Zayas. They hated her family. She hadn't lied when she had applied for this job. She'd just made sure to use her married name. Rio Bella was so small they would have found out eventually, but she had wanted to prove herself so when she told them it wouldn't matter.

If they discovered her family name now, from Kingston, they would see it as a lie and fire her without letting her explain.

Should she go ahead and tell them tonight? Would they listen? Telling them now would be the best. Clearing her mind, she glanced up.

Letti was holding Naomi's hands. "It's way past time to tell him the truth. My brother was wrong in forcing us to keep it secret. I think he was trying to make it right when he left us the ranch."

Naomi shook her head. "I can't even guess why my father is forcing us to work together. But don't tell him, not tonight. Not like this. Let's get him settled in and find the right time. I don't want him to hate us. He just got here."

Abigail blinked. So many of their words matched what was in her head, it didn't make sense. But they were saying *he*. They had to be talking about Kingston.

Not wanting to draw their attention, she backed away slowly. Leo was at home and that was where she wanted to be. Tomorrow was church. She'd turn it all over to God and go from there.

In her car, she turned the key. Nothing. Twice more with the same results. *No. No. No. Why now, God? Please just let me get home.*

She didn't have the time or energy to deal with this. It was probably best if she didn't drive right now anyway. At least her house was less than a mile away if she cut through the flats. With a sigh, she got out and walked into the darkness that surrounded the buildings.

The flashlight on her phone lit the area in front of her. She pulled the fresh night air deep into her lungs and counted to ten before slowly releasing it. At least she would enjoy a good walk. It would help her unwind.

Just a few steps in, she heard rustling behind her. Turning, she swung her phone around, a light blinding her for a second.

"Abigail!" It was Kingston. He jogged to catch up to her. "Where are you going?"

"I'm walking home, Mr. Zayas. I don't live far." She kept moving forward. If she slowed down it would take longer to get home. He was a Zayas and she was a DeLeon. She walked faster.

"When I found your car empty, I was worried." His long strides allowed him to catch up to her with ease. "Glad to see you haven't passed out yet. I have your food. There's a small loaf of handmade sourdough you could eat while you walk." He lifted the bags, then paused and dug into one. He was at her side again in a few steps. "Here. You can eat, and I can apologize for not disclosing my full name." He unwrapped it, tore off a piece and offered it to her.

"Thank you." She bit into the soft bread and moaned. Pausing, she chewed and took another bite. "Seriously. Thank you. I didn't realize how hungry I was." Taking the bag from him, she walked off the graveled path onto a narrow dirt strip. "Since I didn't use my full name to apply for the job, I can't hold that against you either."

"Thanks." There was a short pause. "I won't tell them, you know. Not until you're ready. I promise."

"You should go back." Swallowing another bit, she pointed the loaf ahead of them into the darkness. "If I cut straight across the south pasture and through the flats, I'll be home faster than if I walked on the road."

"Why are you walking?"

"Oh. You know, the typical if-it-can-go-wrong kind of day. My car wouldn't start. But what else did I expect?" The light in her phone went out. "Seriously?" She shook it like that would help. "It's dead."

"Good thing I'm here with a fully charged phone. So, you can follow me." He took her hand and led the way down the narrow deer trail until it split and crisscrossed. He stopped.

"It would have been nice to get it right at least once," he muttered.

"What's wrong?" She took another bite and chewed while waiting to see if he was going to admit he didn't know which way to go.

Maybe it was because she was so hungry, but this was the best bread she had eaten in her entire life. Every guest should have a basket of this bread and cheese waiting for them when they checked in. Maybe with some chips and salsa to keep it Texas. But definitely this bread.

She needed to focus and not dream about event planning and hospitality while standing in the middle of the pasture. At this rate, the sun would be up before she got home. "To get what right?" she asked, despite her resolve to not engage with the enemy. The enemy who knew her secret and could get her fired.

He sighed. "The whole hero thing. I have no clue where to go. I assume you do?"

"That was much faster than I anticipated."

"What?" He turned his gaze from the shadows surrounding them to her.

She couldn't help but grin at his confusion. "The unmanly speed in which you admitted you don't know where to go."

A low, very masculine laugh rumbled through the night air. "I had hoped to play the role of the leading hero tonight, but it seems to have been cut from the script. I'm utterly lost."

She wasn't sure if it was the food or walking, but she was feeling better. She pointed to the left. "We go that way.

The deer, hogs and cattle like making their own trails. And you were already a hero tonight, several times." She waved what was left of the sourdough loaf at him.

"Hogs. Wild hogs with tusks? What about bulls? I've heard you shouldn't go into a pasture with a bull." His light made a wider arch as he swung it around. "Are there any other wild animals?"

"Mainly small ones. Rabbits, raccoons, foxes, possums. A few varieties of snakes."

"Snakes?" He looked at the ground as if expecting to see one under their feet.

"Yes. Another reason boots are a good idea." She might be enjoying this too much. "We also have bobcats, and occasionally a mountain lion or black bear." She had never seen one, but it could happen.

The giant oak tree that stood fifty feet tall and reached out even farther came into view. The gate to her ranch was close by. A shrub on her left moved, and a weak growl came at them from the deep shadow. Or was that hissing? Kingston stepped in front of her with his arm out. "What is that?"

"Not sure." She took his hand and guided the light to the bottom of a dense agarita shrub. The yellow berries were starting to turn red. She bent lower.

Kingston pulled her back. "Careful." He knelt next to her. "What is that?"

A small scruffy dog lay curled around a tiny kitten. The clumps of dried mud made it hard to see what color they were.

"Hey there," she said in a soothing voice as she dropped down beside him. The dog thumped a stubby tail and its lopsided ears perked up. The left one was cut, and dried blood matted the dirty fur. "It's a dog and kitten." She reached under the bush.

He laid a hand on her arm to stop her. "Here, let me." He handed her the phone and took off his jacket.

"Careful, the leaves are hard and pointy like thorns." He was going to tear his very nice shirt. "I can get them."

He was already reaching for them with his jacket. The lining of his fine sports jacket was silk. She had seen this kind of jacket before. Not here, but in Atlanta. Her ex-husband had a collection and would throw a fit if Leo touched it without washing his hands.

"You'll ruin your jacket."

"It can be cleaned or replaced. I don't think picking these guys up with bare hands would be smart." She pulled the branches back to reduce the risk of him getting scratched. Gently, he scooped the two small creatures into his coat.

As he pulled them out, the kitten hissed. The dog licked the ragged ball of fluff and whined as if trying to tell the baby it was okay. "They're both so small. The kitten can't be more than a month old." When she picked it up, it hissed again, and the dog whimpered.

"It's a feisty little thing. How did they get here?" He searched the area as if expecting to find a missing owner.

"Probably dumped at one of the ranch gates." She waved to the roads beyond the pastures and cedar break. "Their ribs are sticking out. They've been out here awhile. I imagine they're dehydrated and might have been trying to get to the river."

"Where are we? I have no sense of direction."

"FM 455 is east of us. That's where the gates to both ranches are located." She pointed in the opposite direction. "The Frio River is west of us, not far. My home is that way, north, and your family's ranch is south."

He nodded and rubbed the wirehaired dog under the whiskered chin. "It looks more like a rat than a dog." He lowered the edge of his jacket. "Here. Give me the little fighter. We need to get you home."

The kitten immediately curled between the dog and man. The purring was so loud the kitten vibrated. "I think she likes you."

"She?" He stepped back onto the path and waited for her.

Holding his phone up, she lit the path for him. "Not sure about the dog, but the kitten is a calico. So, female. First day on the ranch and you have two new pets."

"Pets? Me? No. I'll find homes for them. Maybe take them to the vet first to make sure they're healthy. Do you want them?"

"Oh no. We have too many dogs already. Big ones. The kind that would make a snack out of those two. And it's a no-cat house. My grandfather says he's allergic."

She made her way to the giant oak and the old gate her family had put in generations ago.

"You say that like you don't believe him," Kingston said.

"A few times in school I tried to bring a kitten home and was told that's why I couldn't keep one." They walked in silence as the sounds of the night soothed her. There was only one uncertainty, but she was afraid to ask. "Do you plan on staying on at the ranch for long?" *And are you going to out me before I get a chance prove myself?*

"No, I don't. I have business to take care of in Dallas."

Up ahead, a warm glow guided her home. "We're almost there."

"Juan Carlos bought the Shandly ranch over thirty years ago. How long has your family been here?"

"My family has one of the few original Spanish land grants. There have been six governments that have flown flags over the land. We were here through them all. It's much smaller now than it was back then. Over the decades, families have split it up and sold out. At one time my family, the DeLeons, owned the whole valley. We have a little over nine hundred acres now. We had twelve hundred, but somehow your uncle ended up with about three hundred from my uncle."

"So, my mom was married to your uncle Diego. And somehow a section of your ranch went to my mom, but then it became my grandfather's? How?"

She sighed. "I was four. All I know is the land we just walked across was the part of our ranch my grandfather had deeded to his oldest son, my uncle Diego right before he died. Now the deed is in Juan Carlos's name. How he ended up with it, I don't know." She glanced at him, trying to read his reaction.

"I wasn't even born yet and don't know anything about the land. I know my mother considers Diego the love of her life to this very day. I don't think she ever got over losing him or their baby. Then his family…um." He stumbled over his words.

She assumed he had just realized he was talking to a De-Leon. With the way the Zayases hated the DeLeons, they must have been the villains in Letti's story.

Wait. "Baby? Diego's?"

"Yeah. That's one of the reasons I'm surprised she came here. She always said it had too many painful memories."

"Really?" She had never considered Letti's side of the story. She was about to ask more questions when a very familiar voice interrupted.

"Abby girl?" Her grandfather's rough voice broke through the night. "Is that you?"

"Yes." She glanced at Kingston and for a brief moment wanted to warn him to run. "It's me, Tito."

"What in all tarnation are you doing walking around at

two thirty in the morning? I've been worried. I even tried calling. No telling what those people over there had you doing." He made his way down the steps. For eighty-seven, he was still agile and sharp-witted.

"I'm fine. My car wouldn't start so—"

He froze. "What is he—" her grandfather stabbed a finger toward Kingston "—doing on my property? Zayas, get off my land before I hurt you."

Wide-eyed, she turned to her walking partner. How did her grandfather know Kingston was a Zayas?

Chapter Four

Abigail whipped her head from her grandfather to Kingston. Her protector of wild kittens and savage puppies looked just as confused as she felt. Before she could say anything, her grandfather squared off in front of Kingston. His work-worn weathered hands clinched his hips. If he wore a holster, it would've looked like something straight out of an old Western.

Kingston must've gotten the same vibe. He held one hand in surrender while the other cupped the two rescues close to him. "Sir. I don't know who you think I—"

"I know exactly who you are. You're one of Juan Carlos's brats." He took a step closer, eyes narrowed. "Don't try to deny it. You look just like him. You're all low-down snakes in the grass. You trying to use my granddaughter to weasel your way in? Just like Letti used my son then threw him away. Think again. My land is not yours for the takin', not this time."

"Tito. Please calm down." She put a hand on his arm. "This is Kingston. He just arrived today from Dallas and has been helping me."

Her grandfather spit to the side, keeping his glare on Kingston. "He ain't helping you. They all got an agenda. You never learn, girl. Always trusting the wrong ones."

She flinched. That hurt.

"Sir, I'm just on the ranch to help my cousin and mother, Letti."

Veins throbbed on his wrinkled forehead. "You're her *son*? My family is dead because of Letti and her lies. Get off my land now."

The door opened. "What's going on out here?"

Her oldest brother, Cyrus, stepped onto the porch. He was in the red plaid pajama bottoms she had given him for Christmas. The shirt read Merry Texmas. His thick hair was sticking out in all directions as he rubbed his blood-shot eyes. With the young bulls getting out into the cows' pasture, she knew they'd all had a rough day.

"There's a snake trying to get in our house." Rigo De-Leon was still staring down Kingston like he was a threat to their family and way of life.

Abigail stepped in front of Kingston. "He was kind enough to walk me home in the dark when my car wouldn't start. But Tito is threatening him instead of thanking him." She spoke directly to her grandfather, and she didn't care if she sounded condescending. He was acting like a five-year-old.

"He's the threat." Tito flexed his fingers.

Cyrus sighed and pinched the bridge of his nose.

Lucas came out of the door wearing matching bottoms but with a black shirt. She was sure he only owned black shirts. "Why am I awake at two thirty a.m. and not having fun?" His gaze darted around the yard then stopped on Kingston. "And why is there a man with a dirty rat wrapped in…" He squinted his eyes, as if not believing what he saw. "An expensive-looking jacket? Am I dreaming?" He tilted his head as if to find some sort of clue.

"This backstabbing jackal thinks he can get in good with your sister and then bleed us dry."

"I'm really sorry to cause any trouble." Kingston eased a few steps away from them. "I just wanted to make sure Abigail got home safely and ate." He nodded to the bag of wrapped leftovers she was holding. "I'm going to go now. It was, um, nice meeting you all."

She sighed. "You're not walking. You'll get lost and end up in the river and I'll have to spend my day off looking for you."

He gave her a lopsided grin, and she kind of grinned back.

No. No grinning back. With a stern frown, she lifted her chin. She was tired, that was all. "I'll drive you." She moved to the steps. "Lucas, can I borrow your truck?"

Cyrus shook his head. "You're going inside to eat, then bed. Lucas'll take care of him."

"What? I had a—" Lucas complained, but one glance from their older brother and he turned to the door. "Let me get my keys."

"Tito, take Abigail inside and make sure she eats." Cyrus had been giving them all orders since he'd come home from college at nineteen, giving up his burgeoning baseball career. They had lost both parents, and their grandfather had lost his wife, his daughter-in-law, and both of his sons. She had been four but could imagine Tito had not been in a good mental place to suddenly raise five kids. Cyrus had given up everything to help.

Now pure rage radiated from her grandfather. He kept his glare locked on Kingston as he gripped her hand and led her up the porch.

She was sure her face was red. "Thank you, Kingston. I'll see you at work on Tuesday."

"No, she won't," her grandfather declared.

Lucas came out the door as they were going in. He tossed the keys in the air. "Save some of that barbecue for me. Now that I'm up, I'm hungry. Come on, Zayas. You're going to have to tell me about that." He paused. "Is it a dog?"

The rest of the conversation was cut off as Cyrus closed the door. He watched out the window for a bit then followed them into the kitchen. "Are these the kind of hours they're going to expect you to keep?" Now he was glaring at her.

In all her memories, Cyrus was the head of the family. Even their grandfather leaned on him. Not that it had stopped the two men from butting heads a lot, but Cyrus always got his way.

Being so young when the accident happened, this was her normal. How would their family look if the accident had never happened?

The emotions hitting her tired brain were too much. She needed something else to focus on. She took the containers out and pushed a few buttons on the microwave.

With a sigh, she braced herself to hear all the old arguments again. The million reasons she shouldn't be working at the Tres Amigos Ranch and Resort.

She sat at the family table and waited for the lecture. No point telling them she might not have a job if Kingston told Letti and Naomi she lied on her application. It technically wasn't a lie; her legal name was Harris. But she knew they would have wanted to know her connection to the DeLeon family. Especially now, knowing how hurt Letti felt at the hands of her family.

If she was fired, it would give Abigail's family another reason to hate the Zayases, and they'd like that. She knew they loved her, and all these opinions were just them trying to keep her from getting hurt.

But really, she was a grown woman with a child. When were they going to treat her like an adult? She stopped herself from moaning as she ate the tender beef drenched in the best sauce.

"Well?" Cyrus repeated as Tito grunted.

"I'm not talking about it tonight." She waved her fork at them. "It's been a long day for everyone. In less than five hours we will be up, getting ready for church. You can lecture me then." *Maybe.*

To her surprise, they nodded then left for their bedrooms.

They were right about one thing. It would not be smart of her to get involved with Kingston Zayas on any level. No need to let them get riled up about him. He would be gone before the weather cooled.

Kingston sat in silence as the massive black truck rumbled down the road. The double cab was big enough to sleep in and there were four rear tires, a pair on each side. Lucas must be the rodeo uncle.

The little dog was shaking now. With the saddest eyes ever, she looked up at him and whimpered, as if pleading for something. He rubbed her head. "It's going to be alright."

"What is that thing?" Lucas asked, giving it a side-eye.

"We found them under a bush on the way to your place. They're in bad shape." The kitten meowed.

Not taking his eyes off the road, Lucas grumbled, "Hate it when cowards don't take care of their responsibilities. My sister is good at finding strays. Surprised she didn't bring them in." The big man eyed him as if assessing if Kingston fell into the category of stray or coward.

That was a good question.

He cleared his throat in the awkward silence. "She said

y'all had too many and your grandfather is allergic to cats."
Did she see him as a stray? Was that why she was nice to
him?

They rolled past the big iron-and-stone entrance to Tres
Amigos. "What building are you in?"

"The Live Oak bunkhouse, but you don't need to drive
that far. Just drop me off at the office. It's closer."

"My sister seemed to think you get lost easily." His tone
was dry.

"I can manage a well-lit path." Maybe he didn't know
all the wild animals that lived in the Texas Hill Country,
but he wasn't helpless.

"Thanks for the ride." Kingston opened the door to step
down. A blue light came on, highlighting the step that slid
out from under the carriage. He bet Leo loved that.

"No problem. Oh, and Zayas." Lucas paused until they
made eye contact. He was leaning over the wide console.
"Stay away from Abigail. You met me and Cyrus. There
are two more brothers. Joaquin makes us look small. He's
also the mean one. And Isaac is her twin. She has backup.
Just saying."

What was he supposed to say to that? "Duly noted."

Lucas narrowed his eyes. "Is that a pun about my truck?"

"I, um, don't think so." He didn't want to cause trouble.

"It's a dually." Lucas smirked at him. "Dually noted.
That's funny."

This had been such a weird day. "Well, good night." He
hopped down and closed the door. The chrome step went
into hiding and the light went off.

The pup's whimpering intensified. "Hey, little momma.
It's okay. You and your baby are safe." Farther down the
path was the old foreman's house his mother and cousin
had claimed as theirs. The lights were on.

He paused and considered knocking. But did he want to answer their questions yet? He needed sleep.

As he passed, the door opened and his mother stepped out into the porch light. "You're on the ranch for a minute and you disappear. Where did you go? Was it Abigail? Is she okay?" She raised her eyebrows when the little dog lifted his head. "What is that?"

"They apparently have been dumped."

She came closer to scratch the little dog on the head. "You were always asking for a dog or cat, but we moved around too much. One day on the ranch and you have two pets." Wrinkling her nose, she stepped back. "They desperately need a bath. Come in. There's a utility sink in the washroom. It will be easier than the small sink in the bunkhouse."

She turned and went inside, holding the door open for him.

He went in and waited as she locked the door. The living room and kitchen were one large room with just an island separating them. It was welcoming, with soft floral-printed fabrics on an overstuffed sofa and chairs. Brightly colored Afghans and pillows were everywhere.

"What are their names?" she asked.

"They don't have any." He wasn't keeping them, so why get attached? "Why are you still up? Is Naomi here?" He followed her down a hall.

"Naomi fell asleep in her office. She does that a lot. She wants this ranch to succeed so much. I worry she is going to make herself sick. As for me, I just can't sleep."

"Are you okay?" Days of not sleeping used to be a warning flag that she was about to go off the rails when he was a kid.

She turned on the water and gave him the gentlest smile he had ever seen on her. "I'm so sorry you have to worry about me. I'm in a really good place. Just excited you're here and my brain is twirling with possibilities and a few things I need to take care of. But nothing for you to worry about. I promise." She paused and looked him in the eye. "I'm so sorry about the upheaval I caused in your childhood. I wasn't the best mother."

That was new and unexpected, but not a conversation he wanted to get into tonight. Change of topic. "How are you with being on the ranch? You left the first time after Diego died, right? It must be hard." She had never handled being emotionally challenged well.

"Surprisingly good. I didn't leave Rio Bella willingly back then. I loved this ranch and the town. But you know Juan Carlos. My brother was overbearing and thought he knew best for everyone. He insisted I needed to leave the ranch. I can't believe Diego's been gone for over twenty-five years. I can still hear his laughter." Bubbles covered the tiny dog as she gently washed the clumps of dirt and grime out of her hair. "Maybe I shouldn't have hid from his family, but they hated us and blamed me for all the mistakes he made. I loved him, but he..." Her head dropped and she closed her eyes.

With the kitten tucked under one arm, he put the other around her. "I'm sorry."

She leaned into him and rested for a minute. "Oh, sweet boy. It's ancient history and none of it's your fault." Washing mud out of the tangled fur, she wiped her face with the back of her arm.

He wrapped a towel around the now-shivering dog as his mother took the kitten.

"Losing our baby nearly destroyed me. My last piece of him was gone and his family hated me. My brother knew I needed a reason to live." She patted his face. "He was right. You saved me from completely disappearing into the darkness."

Kingston frowned at that comment. What did his uncle have to do with him? He had so many questions, but it was late, and he didn't think he could process them now.

She took the silence as an invitation to keep talking. "I love you. I have from the moment I heard your little heartbeat. No matter what happens, I want you to remember that."

Well, that was ominous. Unease twisted his gut even tighter than it had been for the last two days. The kitten closed its eyes in bliss as his mother stroked the warm water over the top of its head, washing away the layers of dirt. She didn't look at him, but her voice had a seriousness he wasn't used to. "Tomorrow, you need to come over for dinner and we'll talk." She nodded as if deciding. "The three of us. There's so much to cover."

There was a long pause as she turned off the water. Finally, she met his gaze. "Thank you for coming. I know you're busy with your racehorses. But you have all that computer knowledge. You can upgrade our website." She tucked the kitten into a dark blue towel along with the dog and gave each of them a gentle scratch behind their ears. "I can't tell you how much it means to me that you're here. It was important to my brother that we are here on the ranch together."

But why?

"I had, um, a bit of a problem up in Dallas and I need a place to put one or two of my horses."

"Of course. Is everything okay? Is that why you came now? You're not leaving, are you? You can't leave."

Great. She wasn't going to be happy when he told her he

was just here for a bit. Would they even listen to his proposal for them to buy him out?

Hopefully, they would see how much the horses meant to him and agree to his plan. He didn't belong here.

"We'll talk tomorrow." He'd call Cindy to drive him to town to get boots and jeans. There was also the job of finding a good home for these two orphans.

He knew what it was to feel abandoned and lost. They needed someone who would take care of them permanently. The little dog licked the kitten's ear. Purrs of contentment vibrated through the thick towel and straight into Kingston's chest.

He hugged them closer. "I promise, little momma, I'll find a safe home for you and your baby." He had stopped asking for a pet when he was about seven or eight. The old yearning resurfaced, but it wasn't any more practical now than it was then.

They would be better off with someone else.

"I'll come get you in the morning." Letti passed him and opened the door. When he paused, she leaned up and kissed his cheek.

"In the morning?" he asked.

"Church. You'll love Pastor Banda. Everyone does."

Church? She didn't really mean that. She hadn't gone to church since he was five or six.

"Thanks for washing them."

"I'm going to be here for you. I know in the past I…got distracted and left you to fend for yourself."

A bit of the old bitterness rolled through him. He had needed her as a kid. But he wasn't a kid anymore and he had other things to worry about. The future was where his attention needed to be focused, not the past.

He sighed, gave her a nod and stepped onto the path. The darkness and all the mysteries it held surrounded him.

At the door of the bunkhouse, he turned and looked back. She stood alone. She waved.

He returned the wave and went inside. Tomorrow, he'd tell them his plans and hoped they went along with it.

Something told him it wouldn't be that easy.

Chapter Five

Abigail loved Sunday mornings. As the sun peeked through the curtains her grandmother had made, she pulled crispy bacon out of the oven. Since returning to Rio Bella almost a year ago from Atlanta, she'd made a point to be up early on Sundays and cook breakfast for everyone who was home.

During the week, they were all busy so everyone fended for themselves, but Sunday, whoever was home came to the table before church and she fed them.

Cyrus was pouring coffee for himself, and Tito joined him at the large, worn family table. The two men sat in silence but watched her every move. Were they waiting for the rest of the family to join them before grilling her about last night?

Emma, Cyrus's daughter, came galloping down the back stairs. Leo was laughing, his arms around her neck and his legs hugging her waist. It warmed her heart to see her niece happy. They had lost Charlene to cancer when Emma was only nine years old.

"Careful. That's dangerous," Cyrus scolded them before taking a sip of steaming coffee. The frown was a semi-permanent feature on his face, but she understood. Because of him, she'd got to leave town, go to college, make a go of her dream career, while he had spent his early twenties raising them, then nursing his wife through her treatment.

Cyrus was always putting others first. He had never uttered a single word about his baseball career and stopped any conversation in town when people brought it up. He honored his wife's memory and said he was blessed to share a love and daughter with her.

"Your father's correct." She jumped at her twin brother's voice projected at Emma. Isaac paused under the archway that separated the kitchen from the front living room. His button-up shirt and starched pants were perfectly in place.

He didn't make eye contact with anyone as he sat in the chair that had been his since they had gotten out of high chairs. She had made sure no one else ever sat in her brother's chair.

She had wanted him to be happy and had done whatever she could to prevent a colossal meltdown. Of course, now they understood why. The guilt ate at her that he had gone so long without a diagnosis. After the death of their parents, he had gone completely nonverbal. Everyone said it was grief. It wasn't until college he had received a medical explanation for what was really happening in his brain. At the time she'd had little understanding of the autism spectrum.

"You never run downstairs with someone on your back," he was telling them. "We could end up in the hospital instead of church. I don't want to miss church."

"Sorry, Tio Isaac." Emma let Leo slide down. "It smells so good."

The aromatic scent of pancakes and bacon filled the air as Abigail carefully shaped them into dinosaurs. "Emma, go make sure Lucas knows breakfast is ready."

"Yes, ma'am. What about Tio Joaquin?"

"What about Tio Joaquin?" The second oldest DeLeon

came in from the back door, two big dogs on either side of him. The biggest of her brothers, he filled the door frame. The dogs sat at the door waiting for his next command.

His years as a ranger in the army had given him a stiff spine and weary eyes. It broke her heart that he never smiled. Her older brothers had given up so much to make sure the rest of them had childhoods as stress-free as possible.

"I knew if you wanted to join us for church you would be here. If you didn't, then you would spend your own time with God. Lucas, on the other hand, needs to hear the words from the Good Book as often as possible."

"Amen to that," her grandfather chuckled.

Joaquin came over and kissed her on the side of the head before fixing two plates. He gave one to their grandfather. "Lucas is fine. He just has a different path."

She put a plate in front of Leo and another by Isaac. "Maybe I do too."

"Any path that a Zayas is on is the wrong one," her grandfather muttered.

Isaac frowned. "Why are the pancakes shaped like that?" He pointed at his plate. "They should be round."

Leo's eyes sparkled with anticipation. "Tio Isaac, they're dino-cakes. Momma made them special for me. You don't like them?"

She poured the last of the batter in the sizzling butter.

"Dino-cakes. That is fun. I'm sure they're delicious." Isaac eyed them as if doubting his words, but bless him, he was willing to try.

Cyrus took his plate. "She gave you my plate by accident. These are my dino-cakes." He winked at her. Not quite a smile, but a quirk of his lips followed. She loved her brothers so much. They could be difficult and all of them—even Isaac, who was only ten minutes older—had strong opinions of her life, but she knew it came from wanting the best for her. It was worse since coming home. She blamed the divorce.

"I have yours right here, Isaac." She flipped the round pancakes. Emma came back into the room and made a plate, then sat down next to Leo. "Tio Lucas is on his way."

Abigail passed the plate over the counter and Cyrus handed it to Isaac. Relief flooded his face and his shoulders relaxed. "Thank you for my round pancakes."

Abigail glanced around the table to see if she had forgotten anything. Cyrus had put the jugs of orange juice and milk on the table. Joaquin had added the maple syrup and butter. Isaac had grabbed the bowl of strawberries she had sliced. It was all set.

Tito said, "I'll give him thirty more seconds, then I'm saying the blessing. If he ain't here then he doesn't—"

"I'm here. Sorry. I was up late last night driving our neighbor and his rats to Tres Amigos." He exaggerated a Spanish accent on the ranch's name. "Come home to rest and all I find is drama, little sis."

Isaac frowned. "Rats?"

"Just sit down, boy. I'm hungry and it's getting cold," Tito grumbled. They held hands and bowed their heads as their grandfather prayed over them and their ranch.

After a chorus of amens, there was a sweet moment of silence as everyone ate. These mornings, when every member of her family was here, were rare. Lucas was in for a couple of weeks before he hit the rodeo circuit again. Joaquin was busy working with ranchers in Mexico to build his herds and now he was training service dogs for wounded veterans. As the rookie veterinarian at the local clinic, Isaac was on call most weekends and evenings. Not that he minded.

He preferred the company of animals to people. Always had. And Emma was at an age where she had tournaments or things with friends.

"What happened last night?" Joaquin was the first to speak. "I called Cyrus when I saw all the lights come on, but he said it was handled. Why was Lucas driving people and rats around in the middle of the night? Anything I need to take care of?"

"Did the bulls get out again?" Isaac asked. "I reinforced the gate."

Her grandfather snorted. "There's a young bull that needs to be sent back to Dallas. That kid has no business being here."

Isaac blinked in confusion. He struggled with sarcasm. Leaning closer, Abigail whispered, "He is referring to Kingston Zayas."

"Zayas? We don't trust them." Isaac frowned. "They should not be on our ranch."

"It's no big deal. After we cleaned up the wedding site, my car wouldn't start. I was walking home across the pasture and Kingston was a gentleman and walked me home. We found a small dog and a kitten someone had dumped. He rescued them. That's all it was. He was being nice."

Her grandfather snorted.

"Tito," Leo said after swallowing a bite of his dino-cake. "He was nice when he walked me to Ms. Gloria. I asked if he was related to us, and he said no and he's from far away. I told him he could date Momma and that would make you and Tio Cyrus happy."

"Leo!" After everything that had happened yesterday, one more humiliation was added to her list. It was a surprise that Kingston was nice to her at all. She wouldn't blame him for running in the opposite direction. "You don't say things like that to people you just met."

She glared at her brother and grandfather. "And why is he hearing this kind of talk from you two? I don't need a man in my life."

Her grandfather stabbed an innocent strawberry. "Don't mind that. The Zayas family can't be trusted, period. You have no business being on that ranch."

"Abigail," Cyrus started in, his voice a mix of concern and guilt. "What exactly do you do on that ranch that you need to be there until two thirty? You already worked Monday through Friday."

The rest of her brothers looked just as concerned.

They were broken records, repeating the same line. At least they weren't talking about her love life anymore.

She had plans to fill their ears about them setting her up. It would have to wait until her son was far away.

Abigail took a bite of her pancake, savoring the taste before replying. "It was my first big event. Not only do I love this job, I *need* this job."

Her brothers exchanged skeptical glances. "You're saying the only place you can work is the Zayas ranch?" Joaquin said, raising an eyebrow. "You know they're not to be trusted. And who is this Kingston? What kind of name is that?"

"Kingston isn't a cowboy," Leo piped up. "But he wants to be one. He wears fancy shoes but likes horses. He was really nice to me when Momma got mad."

Cyrus shook his head. "He's not the kind of man your mother should date." He pointed his fork at Abigail. "They need to pay you more if you're going to be working these kinds of hours."

"It was just for the wedding, and I have today and Monday off. I'm good."

Her grandfather nodded slowly. "The Zayases have stabbed us in the back before. It's not wise to get involved with them. They'll use you, then throw you away."

"You've got a degree. Can't you do something else? There's the school and the courthouse," Lucas said around another bite of bacon.

"There's the post office. Willa should be retiring soon," her grandfather told her for the hundredth time.

Abigail held her ground. "If you're so worried about me working the Tres Amigos Ranch, then maybe you'll support me turning our ranch into a venue," she challenged.

There were several degrees of outrage and disgust around the table.

"Until then, I'm staying." She had always worked so hard to smooth things over and be agreeable. It was getting tiring.

Her grandfather cleared his throat. "Abigail," he said, his voice soft, "we just want what's best for you."

"What's best for me is to have a career I love and to take care of my son. I had a great time yesterday. Thanks for asking. The wedding went off without any problems because I was there to organize, plan and reroute. When the couple made their exit, I loved that I had helped make their special day everything they wanted. I've always wanted to do this ever since I was a little girl playing with my Barbies. And I'm doing it on the Zayases' ranch because you won't let me do it here."

There was a moment of silence at Abigail's words. She rarely spoke up or argued with them. Years ago, she learned it was easier to just listen than do what she thought best.

"*Mija*, that family has hurt our family. They are the reason half of us are dead, then they stole our land."

Abigail nodded and reached across her son and Emma to touch her grandfather's calloused hands. "I know, Tito," she said.

"We don't want you to get hurt." Cyrus took his last bite. "If you have to work at that fancy resort they call a ranch, then at least stay away from that kid. You've had enough heartache in your life."

They all had. Maybe her big brother had had it the hardest.

"*That kid* is my age. Since I've come back, you've reverted to treating me as a kid. I'm a grown woman with a child. I know what I want and what I don't want."

She put the empty plates in the sink, then went to Cyrus and hugged his shoulders from behind. "Thank you. But please know I'm perfectly capable of handling myself."

Abigail understood her family's concerns, but she refused to let them dictate her life. "I appreciate all of your advice," she said. "But I've made up my mind. I'm not going to quit my job. And I guarantee you I have no interest in dating anyone, especially Kingston Zayas, and I promise he has absolute zero interest in me." *Not after yesterday.*

"Now, I didn't say not to date anyone." Her grandfather stood. "Rosie's nephew just came into town. He's going to be the head football coach next year. You need to meet a nice boy. One that goes to church. Raising a boy on your own is not the easiest way to live this life."

"Oh, I like football," Leo said, clapping his hands.

She rolled her eyes as she gathered more dirty dishes and put them in the sink. She was definitely going to have a heart-to-heart with the men in her family about playing matchmaker.

"Leo, go wash your hands. I have your shirt on the hook." Once her son was out of earshot, she did her best to give her family the death glare. "I'm going to finish getting ready, then we are leaving for church. And listen to this closely. I'm not interested in dating anyone. No more discussion about my love life or lack of. Not another word."

"That's not what we meant—" Lucas started.

She whipped her hand in front of her closed lips. "Not another word about it." She went to ensure Leo was done and did a last-minute check on herself.

When she went out to the porch, her brothers were waiting by the old tank of a Suburban. She climbed into the back with Emma and Leo.

The twelve-minute drive to church was silent. Not a word was uttered.

She kind of liked it.

Kingston took a slow sip of his coffee. He had watched the sun rise over the tree-covered hills out the kitchen window. He loved this time of the day.

Pounding on the door interrupted the songbirds. Before he could get across the living area, his mother opened the door.

"You're not ready?" She glared, hands on hips. "We're going to be late, and everyone will look at us."

"Late? You were serious about church?"

"Yes." She sighed and looked at her phone. "Go change now and we should make it on time. We don't want to be late. And comb your hair."

She walked over to the rigged dog bed. "How did your pets settle in?"

"Not my pets. I'm finding them a new home."

"Every cowboy needs a dog. Not sure if yours counts,

but it's a start." She grinned at him. "Go change. With all the summer people coming in, it's not real formal so don't worry about what you wear."

Well, that was different. He went into his room that had four sets of bunk beds. Cowboy barracks. He snorted. Another long-buried childhood wish, forgotten. His uncle's offices and game rooms had been full of Western art, making him think the cowboy life would be the best.

That had started his love of horses. Then he'd hung out with Axel's family and the dreams had moved to racehorses.

He looked down at his shoes. He'd texted Cindy an hour ago to set up a time to go into town tomorrow. A new pair of cowboy boots would soon be his.

He joined his mother and followed her to a ranch SUV. "Do you think they'll be alright alone?"

"They'll be fine."

He didn't voice his other question. Would Abigail be at church?

Instead, he asked, "Have you been going to this church long?" Naomi was already behind the wheel. He climbed into the back seat and his mother got in the front.

"When we first arrived, we were driving to Uvalde to a bigger church. But we thought it would be better to come into town to build goodwill locally. Everyone's very gracious in a bless-your-heart kind of way. They keep their distance though. Our family doesn't have the best reputation in town. But we want to change that."

Naomi nodded in agreement.

"So, Abigail's family's not the only one that hates us?" Utility poles, pastures dotted with cattle, horses and goats streamed past them. The sky was an overcast gray.

His mom looked confused. "Abigail's family hates us?"

Oh man. He wanted to punch himself in the face. "She

loves y'all and working on the ranch is the best job she's ever had." He hoped he wasn't overselling it. "Just her family has given her grief working for Zayases. That's all I know. She said something about it while we were working last night." He needed to stop talking.

"Unfortunately, thirty years ago, when Juan Carlos bought the ranch from the bank, some people in the area blamed him for the destruction of the family that had lost the land. And they think we are destroying the authentic hill country with our new fancy ideas." Letti air quoted the end of her statement.

"Many of the locals still refer to it as the Shandly ranch. Seems the smaller the town, the bigger and longer the grudges," Naomi added.

"Then there's Diego and his family's accusations." His mother closed her eyes and sighed. "I should have just given that parcel of land back to them, instead of signing it over to my brother. Juan Carlos said Diego owed him and I wasn't very good at standing up to my brother." She rolled her head to the side and looked at Naomi. "Maybe we're pushing a boulder up a hill, and it's just going to roll back and flatten us."

Naomi reached across and patted Letti's hand. "The clientele for the resort isn't the locals. Our best markets are folks from large cities looking for an authentic Western ranch experience."

"I know." But his mother sounded sad and a little defeated. "But the people we hire will mostly be local. I want us to become a part of this community and to have a positive impact on Rio Bella. I've always loved this town. I want it to love me back."

"And you do that by going to church?" For some reason that explanation disappointed him. It was too close to the hypocrisy of the rest of the family. He might not go to church, but in his core, he believed it should fill a spiritual calling, not a way to grow a business.

His mother frowned as they turned at an intersection. A large sign surrounded by huge blocks of limestone and wildflowers welcomed them to Rio Bella.

"I guess that's part of it. But for me it's fellowship. My faith is important to me. It changed my life and led me to self-awareness and grace. Especially when it comes to our family and how I raised you."

Naomi glanced over at him, then to the road. Her fingers went up in a wave to a passing car. "What about you? Where does your faith stand?"

The tires crunched over red gravel as she pulled into an already-full parking lot.

He leaned back and looked at the white steeple. Stained glass windows gleamed in a straight line down the side of the clapboard-and-limestone building. A burnt orange Suburban told him Cindy was here. Look at that, he already knew someone.

"Kingston?"

Where was his faith? "That's a good question." He'd been asking himself that lately. He was good at smiling and giving people what they wanted, but it left him not really knowing himself. "I'm not sure." He pulled the handle, then glanced between the two women.

"I'm glad your faith helped you, Mom. Thanks for inviting me." He studied the picture-perfect country church. So much had gone wrong since his difficult childhood, and now the fire that threatened his lifelong dream. Could a small-town church in the middle of nowhere really have answers for him?

He stepped down and bumped into Abigail DeLeon.

Chapter Six

~~~~~~

"Sorry." Kingston stepped back and couldn't help but smile at her. His day was already looking better. Today, her hair was in a neat ponytail. A soft yellow dress with little flowers flowed around her. The light pink glasses she wore had more flowers at the corner. Who knew glasses could be so pretty? She must be feeling better this morning.

Her head was down as she dug in her duffel-size purse. Looking up, an apology died on her lips. Her eyes went wide.

"Momma!" Leo ran from across the yard. He grabbed her hand. "Can I sit with Matthew? His mom said it was okay."

"Hey, Leo." He had never really noticed kids before, but he liked this little guy. And a good reminder of why he had decided to keep his distance from Abigail. He wouldn't want to let him down.

"Hi, Mr. Kingston." Leo's smile stretched impossibly wide. Then he frowned and glanced at his mom. "We're not supposed to talk to him."

Kingston raised an eyebrow at her.

She flushed, took a deep breath and opened her mouth, but didn't say anything.

Leo moved closer to his mother. With worry on his face, he glanced between the two adults. "I shouldn't tell Tito you're with Mr. Kingston, right?"

"I'm not with Mr. Kingston. We just happened to be in the parking lot at the same time. I went to the car to find my ChapStick." She sighed. "We can say hi to Mr. Kingston. And you are sitting with me and—"

"Hi, Abigail," Kingston's mother said as she and Naomi came up next to him.

Abigail's face transformed with her smile, even though it was a little off. "Good morning. Sorry I disappeared without speaking with you last night. My brothers are going to check on my car later this afternoon. Were your friends happy with the wedding?" She gave Kingston a nervous glance, then looked down at her son. "You know what? Today you can sit with Matthew."

"Yay! Thank you." He ran off.

Kingston tried to reassure her that he hadn't said anything to them about her family. Well, other than the comment that slipped out about her family hating them, but fortunately the whole town seemed to have a problem with the Zayas family. He grimaced. That wasn't a pleasant thought.

"Don't apologize," Naomi said. "You should never have been working that late. Car problems are the worst. If there's anything I can do to help, let me know." Naomi stepped forward, taking Abigail's hand in hers. "As far as the Dillons' wedding, they loved every moment and gave me a cash tip to pass on to you. You can stop by and pick it up anytime. We have another wedding in a couple of weeks, so make sure you're rested. Hopefully, it will get easier as we get more experienced."

"See you inside." Letti looped her arm through Naomi's and headed toward the church doors. They stopped at the end of the sidewalk to allow an older couple to go ahead of them.

Abigail gave Kingston a worried glance, then smiled. "You didn't say anything about my name. Thank you." She adjusted her purse. "I better get in there before my brothers send a search party for me."

"Can't be caught consorting with the enemy?"

"You don't know how close to the truth that is."

He looked at the double doors. A rolling wave of caterpillars turned in his stomach. Why did entering a church make him nervous? It was just a building.

Matching his steps with Abigail's, he studied her. "How do you plan to keep your secret while going to the same church? It's a pretty small town, if you hadn't noticed."

Taking a deep breath, she nodded. "I'm going to explain who I am first thing Tuesday. So, you don't need to worry about covering for me. I don't like keeping secrets. I'll see you later."

She turned and fled inside the double doors. With no excuse for standing alone on the sidewalk, he followed her.

The small lobby opened into a much larger space than he had anticipated. His gaze was immediately drawn up to the dark, curved beams that crisscrossed above them.

The polished wood pews curved to create a semicircle leading to the altar. He saw Abigail heading to the front right side. A couple of her brothers saw him and glared as she slipped into the pew behind them.

Not knowing what else to do, he nodded and smiled.

Letti waved him over. She and Naomi were sitting in the next to last pew to the left. Not in the front. That was good. And bonus point, because he could see the DeLeon family, but they couldn't watch him without turning around. It worked for him.

"Kingston!" He turned and Cindy engulfed him in a hug. "Welcome. I think you'll love Pastor Banda. Each week, I'm moved by the words he shares with us. When our hearts are open to the word of God, it has the power to change our lives. Hello, ladies."

She moved on to greet others.

"Look at you already making friends. Not everyone hates us." His mother smiled at him. "You're good with people."

"It's a skill I learned to survive." He regretted the words as soon as they left his mouth.

Her smile was gone, and her gaze went to the worn Bible in her hands. "Our life was complicated. Give the ranch and town a chance. You might find you can build a home here."

Home. Was she talking about giving *her* a chance? His gaze went to the DeLeon family. He wouldn't be here long enough to make it a home. He wasn't sure he knew what *home* meant. Abigail's family were a little rough, but they seemed to have a good grasp of the concept. He couldn't even begin to imagine four generations living together by choice—and happily.

Abigail leaned in to listen to the older woman beside her. She nodded and smiled. Was she as real as she seemed?

Lucas caught him watching and his eyes narrowed, his top lip pulling up at the corner. Was he growling at him? Kingston wasn't sure what to do. He didn't want to be the first to back down, but he didn't want to start anything either. With a smile, he gave him one quick nod then turned to his mother.

"You need to leave Abigail alone. It's hard enough being a single mom," she whispered. "We already have enough trouble with the locals. We can't afford to lose her."

"What do you think I'm going to do?"

"I see the way you watch her. You just met yesterday. She's the kind of person people are drawn to. Makes her great at her job." She grinned, then bit her lip. "I want the best for you. I always did." Were her eyes tearing up?

He wanted it to be true. There would be a hard decision coming his way soon.

"You deserved a better mother. Now face forward and keep your eyes on the pastor."

"Yes, ma'am." There was something much deeper going on here than he had anticipated. Everyone stood and a woman with a guitar led them in a song.

He gave Abigail one last glance as he listened to the music. The words surrounded him and lifted his gaze up. *God, is this where You want me? Do You even care about me and my life?*

Could he truly trust that God cared and loved him completely? Kingston Zayas. There was no way he was lovable. His own mother had forgotten him more than once.

When the service finished, his gaze moved to the dust particles dancing in the light flooding through one of the stained glass windows. Behind the altar, Jesus stood with his arms open, hands out. Inviting.

Was this feeling real? He needed air.

Naomi bumped him with her shoulder. "Earth to Kingston."

People were leaving. The pastor stood at the opened doors, shaking hands. "Sorry."

"Letti went to the ladies' room." A gentle hand touched his and her golden-brown eyes were full of concern. "Are you okay?" Of all their family, they were the only two with the exact same color eyes.

He grinned, trying to shake off the feeling that his life had just changed. "I don't know. I'm ready to head home. Not sure how much longer I can trust the dynamic duo alone." *Home.* There was that word again.

"Those two survived alone in the wilderness. I think they can manage a few hours in a comfy bed."

"That's what Mom said." But they shouldn't have had to endure that trauma. They needed extra care now. Following Naomi, they stopped to speak to the pastor. Well, she spoke. He just stood there, then shook his hand.

Outside, Naomi crossed the grassy yard and headed straight for Abigail. What was she doing? He hesitated. But standing alone in the middle of the yard was foolish. With a sign, he walked with as much false confidence as he could gather.

What was his cousin up to? If she saw the family together, it would probably expose Abigail before she had the opportunity to tell them she was a DeLeon.

He needed to derail Naomi. "Hey, let's go wait for Mom at the car." He gently tugged on her arm. But there was no stopping her. Abigail's eyes were wide, and she glanced at him in a panic.

Abigail watched her son run off with Sylvia and Matthew. It wasn't that long ago he didn't want her out of his sight. But he was gaining confidence and developing friendships. She wasn't going to allow sadness to take hold of her. His independence was good for both of them.

Turning, she noticed one of her bosses walking toward her, Kingston trailing behind. He flashed her a look of apology. Her heart slammed against her rib cage.

Had he told Naomi during church? She glanced around. Her brothers and her grandfather surrounded her. *No, not now.*

The men in her family had varying degrees of frowns or scowls. If she'd had enough elbows, all of them would be sporting bruises. She stepped forward to separate herself from her family. A cowardly thing to do, but she had nothing else. "Hi, Naomi."

"Hello. I was wondering if you wanted to join us for lunch."

So, he hadn't told her.

"What?" Cyrus nearly growled as he came up behind her. "You want to make Abigail work more hours for you?"

Naomi's smile wavered. "Excuse me?" Her brow furrowed in confusion.

Tito snorted as he joined the fun and stepped in front of Abigail. "No." He jabbed a finger at her boss. "We won't excuse you. And keep that boy away from her." A weathered hand waved in Kingston's direction.

Kingston grabbed his cousin's arm. "I see Mom. Let's go."

Naomi pulled her arm free. "Wait. Are you Abigail's family?" Her gaze jumped between the men and Abigail before turning to Kingston. "Did you know this was her family?"

He sighed in utter defeat.

Abigail couldn't stop the groan or the impending disaster. She stepped around her grandfather and tried to shoulder him back.

"You're related to Rigo DeLeon?" Naomi's normally gracious voice was sharp. "Do you know what he put my aunt through?"

Lucas chuckled. "If you're inviting her to lunch, I think we should all come." He winked at Naomi and Cyrus elbowed him.

"What, so she can poison us all?" her grandfather snarled.

"She could," her twin said. "There are several poisons in the Texas Hill Country."

"Isaac. She's not going to poison us." Abigail cut off her

twin before he started listing the plants by their proper Latin names.

"Humph. Says you," Tito mumbled. "Wait. I guess she can't do that until her boy is married to our Abigail. That way they can get what's left of our ranch."

Heat crawled up her neck. It would be red soon. "I'm so sorry. Please ignore them. Rigo is my grandfather. Harris is my married name. These…men, for lack of a better term, are my brothers. I wasn't trying to hide anything. I just thought it would be…"

"You didn't tell her you were a DeLeon?" Joaquin blinked in confusion. Like she was ashamed of them, and he couldn't understand why.

She ignored the men in her family and stepped closer to Naomi. "I'm sorry. I really like working for you. I wanted to show you I was more than my name, that's all. I would love to have lunch. Unfortunately, I can't today. There's a community fundraiser at the school. You should go." *Positive. Stay positive.* "Plates are ten dollars, and one hundred percent goes to funding a new playground."

She glanced at Kingston for help. He nodded. "Mom's already in the car. The fundraiser sounds like a good idea."

Abigail kept her hands down to stop them from rubbing her forehead at the headache forming. Focused on her boss, she smiled. "Please join us. You haven't been to any community events yet. It's a good place to be seen, and your money is going for a good cause."

Naomi's gaze traveled over the men in her family, then the people milling around. She planted a diplomatic smile on her face and nodded. "Sounds nice."

Abigail glanced at Letti, already in the car, apparently hiding from them all.

Good call. She wished she had been faster.

Cindy rushed over, cutting through the tension. "Naomi and Abigail! I'm glad you haven't left yet. Did y'all hear that black mold was found in the fellowship hall? All Wednesday night dinners are canceled. They are also trying to figure out if they'll be forced to cancel Vacation Bible School in two weeks." She glanced between Naomi and Abigail. "I thought a venue owner and an event coordinator might have an idea where they could go." She winked at Kingston.

He stepped back. "That's a lot of kids running around."

"Oh, no. It's very organized. Y'all wouldn't have to do anything but provide the space. Your event barn would make a perfect central location. We already have all the volunteers and supplies. We just need a location. It's Monday through Friday. We would get there around eight, the kids arrive at nine and everyone is gone by one—well, other than Monday and Friday when we do a big cookout. You could use your normal fee as a write-off. What do you think?"

Naomi smiled. "I think it's a great idea. Let me talk with Letti and our amazing event coordinator." She nodded to Abigail. "Can I call you tonight around six to confirm and get more details?"

"Yes. Yes. This will be great."

Abigail let out all the tension from her stiff muscles. She had admitted the truth, and she hadn't lost her job. "It will give people an opportunity to see what we're doing with the ranch."

"Yes! Thank you so much." Cindy hugged Naomi and Abigail before bouncing off.

Her boss blinked a couple of times. "Well, that was interesting."

Her grandfather snorted. "They could use our ranch. Why are they going over there, to the interlopers?" With a suspicious glare, he leaned toward Naomi. "You trying to weasel your way into our community? It ain't going to work this time. There's enough of us who remember what your family did."

Naomi glowered. "You have a fuzzy memory. My father bought the Shandly ranch fairly. Then your son ran off to gamble away the money my father gave him. He abandoned his wife. Then you blamed her." There was so much pain in Naomi's eyes. Pressing her lips into a tight line, she straightened her spine. "She needed you and you slammed the door in her face. Please leave my family alone. We have every right to be here. You stay on your side of the fence, and we'll stay on ours."

"Well, that's the problem, ain't it? You're the ones standing on our land," he said between clenched teeth.

Isaac shook his head. "Tito, you were the one who signed over part of the ranch to Tio Diego. He left it to his wife. She signed it over to her brother. I checked at the courthouse. It's all legal."

"That don't make it right. That woman tricked him. Juan Carlos set him up." He pointed to the car. "It was all her fault."

Kingston stepped in front of the accusing finger. "No. She loved Diego. I think she still does. Any choices he made were his own. Stop blaming her. She had nothing to do with the accident."

"You don't know what you're talking about. It's all lies." Her grandfather's breathing was as fast as if he had been running. He slashed his hand through the air. Cyrus and Joaquin looked at each other over their grandfather. With a nod, Joaquin placed one arm around the older DeLeon's shoulders and a hand on his arm to gently guide him to their dark grey Suburban.

People were whispering. Abigail's own breathing was labored. Thankfully, Leo wasn't witnessing this.

Abigail wanted to cry. This was not how she'd wanted her boss to find out her maiden name.

Kingston's throat visibly moved when he swallowed. "I'm sorry for reacting the way I did. I know how much my mom was hurt when... By everything that happened. She loves it here and just wants a new start."

Abigail nodded. "I understand coming home and wanting a new start." He had just been defending his mother. The image of him holding the abandoned pets in the expensive jacket needed to be shoved out of her mind, but it was melting into her heart. *Nope. No. Nope.*

She had fallen for her ex-husband when he had given her his umbrella to keep dry in the pouring rain. One gentlemanly act didn't mean he was a keeper. In the end, her husband's career had been more important than her or their son. Just like Kingston was focused on his business in Dallas.

Right now, her son had to be her focus.

Naomi took her hand. "I'm so sorry about the drama. Our family history is painful and messy. No one was left unscathed. How old were you when the accident happened?"

"Four. I don't remember much. There are lots of pictures, but no one talks about it. Other than how the Shandlys lost their ranch, and Diego lost the south pasture that you now own." She had applied for the job not knowing what to expect from the Zayas women. But she liked them and saw how hard they were working to make the ranch their home and livelihood.

There was no way she could tell her grandfather and brothers that she identified with these women and felt she belonged on their ranch as much as she did the DeLeon ranch.

Naomi must have seen the guilt and torment because she pulled her in for a hug. "It's going to be okay. I understand why you used your married name." She stepped back and lifted her brows while she gave Abigail a teasing smirk. "You're not a spy sent in to discover our secrets, are you?"

With a laugh, Abigail shook her head. From the corner of her eye, she noticed Cyrus leaning against the Suburban, arms crossed.

Kingston cleared his throat. "We should be going."

Naomi smiled at Abigail. "See you at the fundraiser." She turned and walked to her car. Hands in his pockets, Kingston gave Abigail a quick nod then followed.

They walked with the exact same mannerisms.

A nudge on her shoulder drew her attention to her family. Lucas was closest to her and smirking.

"What?" she asked.

"You like him. That's going to cause lots of trouble."

"I do not!" Realizing her voice was a little pitchy, she lowered it. "I have no interest in Kingston Zayas."

"Mmm-hmm." He just grinned.

"I was just thinking they had the same walk with the exact same gait. Letti doesn't. They must take after Juan Carlos. They have the same color eyes too. Do you remember meeting him?" She hitched her purse higher on her shoulder.

"Nope." He narrowed his gaze and looked off into the distance. "Wait. I do remember him coming to the house after…well, after. It started out fine, then he and Tito started yelling and almost got into a fight. Cyrus jumped between them. Joaquin called the sheriff. Think both Letti and Naomi were with him. Naomi was about fifteen at the time. Letti was crying. I ran to my room. It was too much. I was still… Well, you know."

She wanted to cry for him, but he would hate that, so she settled for a brief side-hug. Did her family know about Letti losing her uncle's baby? That was too personal, and it wasn't her place to say anything if her family didn't know. "Letti's my boss and I like her. Don't worry about Kingston. He's temporary. I have no interest in him." Without a doubt, he had no interest in her.

He laughed as he opened the back door for her. "You keep saying that."

Sometimes, she really hated her brothers.

Chapter Seven

❧

Kingston glanced at his watch. His Monday morning ride should be here soon. The burnt orange Suburban would be taking him to town to purchase much-needed boots and jeans. Making sure to get the horses out, neither he nor Axel had gone upstairs. If it hadn't been on his back or in Axel's truck it was lost in the fire. A comfortable shirt would also be welcomed.

Then again, he could cancel and go back to bed. Sleep was still something he hadn't managed much of. His meeting with his mom and Naomi about his plan hadn't happened, because Axel had arrived while they were all at the fundraiser. Kingston had rushed to the ranch and together they'd settled Fuego, Kingston's prized racehorse, in a small pasture close to the stables.

It had taken hours of settling the stallion before they could leave him alone. In the bunkhouse, they'd stayed up even later as Axel updated him on where they stood with the insurance and how the other horses were doing. Cielo and Flyer would keep to their race schedule, but Oceano would need some extra time to recover.

Axel had gotten a kick out of Little Momma and Baby. He grinned. Seemed they had names now. But it was temporary.

Before the sun was up, Axel had been on the road to Dallas and the other horses. He'd tried to get some sleep, but a hurricane of thoughts and worries had kept him up.

Until yesterday, he had not fully comprehended the emotional and intense situation with the DeLeon family. Rigo DeLeon actually believed his mother and uncle had stolen the piece of land between the ranches. What did they think their motive was? They hadn't sold it, and until this year they had just leased it out for pastureland.

Right on the hour, the burnt orange Suburban made its way down the long drive. He yawned.

His phone chimed with a text. His mother wanted to know how Fuego was and when Kingston was coming over to chat. He closed his eyes and groaned. With a short reply he apologized, telling them he would meet them later.

No response. Great. Now guilt would nag at him. Should he just tell Cindy he'd go another time? The Suburban slowed down as it approached. There was someone else in the front seat. He narrowed his gaze. He thought it would be a solo trip. Did Cindy double-book? He wasn't in the mood for making small talk.

She drove a little past him then parked. Abigail sat in the passenger seat. *No way.*

He opened the back door. "Thought you had the day off."

An exaggerated smile stretched across her face. "*Hola* to you too."

His phone chimed. Sounds good. Have some stuff to do this morning. Talk over early dinner?

He replied with a thumbs-up, then got in. So much easier than the third row he'd ridden in from the airport.

He looked up and Abigail was staring at him, brow lifted. She wore square purple glasses today.

Why did he always seem to be at his worst around her?

"Sorry. I was answering a text from my mom and I didn't mean to be rude. Good morning. I didn't know this was a rideshare."

"Do you want me to get out?" She leaned into her seat but turned her gaze forward.

"Don't be ridiculous. I was just surprised." He hesitated, then decided to admit the truth. "I'm glad it was you."

"I guess I should have warned you, but I never say no to a paying customer." Was there a twinkle in Cindy's eyes? "I didn't think it would be a problem since you already know each other."

"No problem." He bit back a smile and clicked his seat belt. "Abigail, what has you using the local taxi?" His mood was lighter, and he really wanted to smile. It had nothing to do with her. It didn't. *Liar!*

He was in so much trouble.

"No car." Turning around, she met his gaze, but one brow was curved high. "I have business to take care of in town. Leo wanted to ride the fence with Joaquin. My brothers couldn't fix my car so it's in the garage. So here I am." She twisted farther to look at him more directly. "I hear you are going into town to get real working gear. Need help picking things out?"

"Um. Cindy said she could help."

"Nope," his driver said as she pulled off the ranch road onto the highway. "Got a job picking up a delivery in Uvalde. First stop, Rio Bella Saddlery and Supplies where you can get the best boots in the state. Then I suggest the mercantile or the feed store for hats, jeans and pet stuff. The courthouse is across the street. Y'all can have lunch at The Nest, and I'll pick you up there."

Kingston tugged on his ear. He'd never had a driver give him orders before. "I don't need to go to the courthouse."

"That's for me. I have a ticket to pay. You don't have to follow me. It's a small town. If you get lost, just ask someone where The Nest is and you can wait there."

"I'm not going to get lost." He sounded like a child. "Wait. You have a ticket? For what?"

She shrugged as if she didn't care.

"And don't worry about carrying stuff around," Cindy said before he could press Abigail for more information. "Just leave it at the counter and tell them I'll be by to pick it up."

After that, the rest of the trip into town was quiet except for the praise music playing on Cindy's battery-operated device for her CDs from the 1990s. He grinned.

As they approached the small town, Cindy slowed. The corner store on the edge of Rio Bella was the only modern building and hosted the lone fast-food chain available in town.

There wasn't a single traffic light, just one flashing red light warning of a four-way stop.

Cindy pointed to the left. "That's The Nest, the oldest café in the canyon."

It looked like a diner out of an Edward Hopper painting. Cindy was still talking. "Billy O'Bryan came from New York City and opened the restaurant at the end of World War II. His granddaughter, Linda, and her son run it now. Best breakfast and burger in the county. He passed a few years ago."

The family had been here since the forties and were still considered to be from New York? No wonder it was hard for Naomi and Letti to become part of the community.

Playing tour guide, Cindy pointed out more highlights along the main street. The buildings were an eclectic mix of architectural influences. Many were made of huge blocks of local limestone. Others were colorful storefronts and a few were painted cinder blocks. Trucks and SUVs lined the main street, making it a busy and popular place.

The car pulled into a small gravel parking lot. "I'll give you a call when I leave Uvalde. It's about an hour trip."

Kingston got out and moved to the slightly uneven sidewalk. He wasn't sure where to begin. Across from them was the large limestone courthouse, which was surrounded by huge oak trees that looked as if they had been here long before any Europeans had settled the area. There was a store with women's clothes in the window, a flower shop and a lumberyard. Where was the boot place?

"Do you need help?" Abigail was facing him, but he couldn't see her eyes now that she had replaced her purple glasses with oversize bright blue sunglasses. She was probably looking at him as if he was a giant toddler.

"I'm sure I can figure it out."

She had a soft laugh. "Come on. We'll start at the Saddlery for boots. Carter has a mix of handmade boots and some from the leading brands." She took his hand and led the way.

Her touch was soft and warm. She led him through a door and a bell chimed like in an old movie. He grinned.

The scent of leather surrounded him. In the shop window, there were several Western saddles, but here in the store an assortment of leather products were hanging on a wall or piled in bins. One wall was floor-to-ceiling boots.

"Hi, Abigail. Good to see you. Did you come in to finally buy that saddle you've been eyeing?" A man younger than he'd expected sat behind the counter, working on something.

"Good morning, Carter. No. My grandfather would not appreciate a new saddle at the ranch. My friend here is looking for some good work boots. He just arrived at the Tres Amigos."

The man stopped what he was doing and looked over his glasses at Kingston. He raised his eyebrows. "You're the new wrangler or the new Zayas?"

Stepping forward with his hand outreached, he smiled. "Kingston Zayas. Nice to meet you. I'll need gear to be ready to do whatever my mother and cousin need done."

Carter stood and nodded. He walked around the counter with a slight limp and shook his hand. "Welcome to Rio Bella. Do you want real working boots or dress boots?"

"Maybe both. I need a good pair of boots that will get through all the operations of a ranch. I'll also be working with the horses, even though I'm not the new wrangler." He now knew the wrangler on a ranch was in charge of the horses. He liked that idea. "I do have years of experience with horses, but none on a ranch."

"Really?" Abigail sounded surprised.

"I own a few racehorses. One of them arrived at Tres Amigos last night."

The man went to the wall of boots. "I have just the pair." He glanced at his feet. "Eleven or twelve?"

"Eleven and a half if you have it. If not, twelve will work."

Carter pulled down a few pairs of boots. "See if they're comfortable."

Abigail pulled some for him to try, and he ended up with two new pairs of boots. Carter seemed pleased when the first pair Kingston picked were handmade by him, the store owner.

While he paid, Abigail studied the saddles then smiled when he joined her. They waved to Carter then stepped outside into the bright sun and made their way along the wide sidewalk.

"Next stop, a hat, jeans and shirts. Might need some new socks too. Not sure yours would hold up under ranch conditions. But then again, you might not be here long enough to do any real damage."

She brought her gaze up to his. "I meant to the socks. Not um…" She waved her hand around as if it covered the rest of the sentence. "Wait. If you work with horses, why are you starting from scratch? You should have most of this stuff."

He let out a heavy sigh. "I lost everything in a fire last week."

She stopped in the middle of the sidewalk. "What?"

"We had bought a solid barn and turned the loft into an apartment. I lived there with my partner."

"Partner?" How had she not known he had a partner?

"Business partner and best friend. He grew up in a family that worked and trained racehorses. We wanted to have our own. Not easy, which is why we spent our savings on a place to put the horses, then found a way to live there too. Saved money for the horses, at least until the fire. We have four. Two had promising starts before us, but people had lost faith in them, so we picked them up for a lot less than they're worth. The plan is to turn them around and make them contenders and breed our own line. Earlier last week, we came home from an event to find the tack room on fire. We got the horses out but lost everything."

"You saved the horses. Where are they now?"

"Hawthorn Stables, where Axel's dad works. Axel is my partner. He worked there until recently. I had a job working on computers all day. Saved up for a few years and we were having a go at it full-time, but then the fire. Fuego had the worse reaction. He just arrived at Tres Amigos yesterday so I can work with him."

"That's why you showed up suddenly with very few clothes. I thought you were just a light traveler." She grinned at him then faced forward and started walking again, her serious face back in place. "You won't be staying."

"I haven't told my mom and Naomi everything yet. The conversation was going to happen last night, but Fuego arrived. Axel and I had business to discuss. I'm going to talk to them later today."

"Letti and Naomi think you are here because of Juan Carlos's will. It might not be any of my business, but they're so excited you're here."

"Which is one of the reasons I kind of put it off. My mom is doing so well. I've never seen her so…well-adjusted, filled with a purpose. If I don't stay at the ranch, then they'll be fifty-fifty partners. They don't need me." He didn't like talking about himself. "Why don't you get the saddle you want?"

She snorted. "Have you seen the price of Carter's saddles? Each one is worth it, but not in my budget."

They crossed a small side street that connected to Main. The next building was long with tin siding and white window frames. *Fernando's Feed and Seed* was in bold cursive lettering on the side. At the front of the store, a line of heavy wooden posts held up a tin covering that extended over a worn, whitewashed boardwalk.

Three old cowboys sat under the deep overhang. They were playing a game of dominos on a table that looked as if it was made from the same wood as the decking. The building took up two whole blocks with three silos and a loading dock.

It looked like something from a movie set.

"Good morning, gentlemen. How's the game going?" Abigail rested her hand on one of the chairs and leaned in to study the game.

"Hank's cheating," the oldest-looking cowboy grumbled.

"Nope. Just finding the best strategy to win. What's the point of playing if you ain't trying to win?" the one that was probably Hank argued.

"How's your granddaddy doing? He should join us and let you young guns to do the heavy lifting."

"You know he'll just say if he sits too long death will find him." She waved toward him. "This is Kingston Zayas. These troublemakers are Hank, Pete and Fernando of Fernando's Feed and Seed. His granddaughter does the heavy lifting now."

All three men glared at him. Fernando turned to her. "Does Rigo know you're fraternizing with a Zayas?"

"Heard there was a showdown at church yesterday." Hank narrowed his eyes as he studied Kingston.

She rolled her eyes. "You know everything is exaggerated around here. Be nice. Might be a paying customer. He's looking for working gear and all the things a small dog and kitten would need."

"Actually, I'm hoping to find a new home for them." He studied the bulletin board covered with layers of help-wanted and for-sale flyers. "They were dumped at the ranch. Is there a no-kill shelter in town? Or a place I can post about finding a good home for them?"

All three men laughed. "If you want to make sure they stay alive then you're their home," Pete said.

Hank shook his head. "Hate cowards that dump poor animals. So, you takin' them in?" He stared over his glasses in the most judgmental stare Kingston had ever encountered, and that was saying a lot. First Lucas, and now these men.

Abigail turned to him. The expectation he found in her gaze did something to his gut. He couldn't bear to let her down. Not wanting to disappoint people made life so much more difficult.

He wouldn't be here long enough to give them a home. Why didn't she understand that?

"Got everything you need for your new pets. You want real cowboy gear or a fancy play outfit?" Fernando broke the silence as he laid a domino down. Apparently, the matter of finding a home for the dog and cat was settled.

Hank cleared his throat. All four were waiting for an answer.

"Real ones." He pulled his mouth to the side. "I don't like fake."

"A lot of the city folk prefer the fake ones." Two of the men chuckled. "So was Juan Carlos your father?"

"He was my uncle. Letti, his sister, is my mom."

"The one who married Diego?" Two of the cowboys pushed their hats back and raised their brows.

"Yes, but I was born a little over a year after he died. Just to be clear."

Fernando grunted and took a drink of coffee. "Juan Carlos didn't buy local. You new Zayases going to change that?"

"I'm buying local right now. I'll send Naomi your way and you can talk to her. She oversees the buying of supplies." He looked at his watch. "Don't you need to go to the courthouse?"

Abigail's eyes went wide. "I do. Let's get you taken care of then I can run over to the courthouse."

"You better pay that ticket, girl. Your grandfather would have a fit if you got yourself arrested in the middle of town.

And you know Jasper would do it just to mess with your brother."

"Let's go so these gossips can talk about good people." She grabbed his hand and took him into the store.

"You don't seem like the kind to break rules, let alone laws."

"A couple of times I went over the speed limit to make sure I got to school on time to pick up Leo. Jasper has a grudge against Lucas and loves causing trouble for any DeLeon whenever he gets the opportunity."

"So, it's not just my family they have feuds with? And why would you get arrested for a traffic ticket?"

"It was due three months ago and until recently I didn't have the money."

"You didn't pay your ticket?"

She sighed. "Sometimes the choices are Little League fees and shoes for your kid or paying tickets."

Right, she was a single mom. "What about his dad? Shouldn't he help? At least with the shoes and stuff."

"He's starting his own business and says he never wanted kids for this very reason. It's easier to just deal with it on my own."

"But he does have a son. The court doesn't—" Her glare cut him off.

"I don't like conflict. He sends money when he can. Let's take care of you and your new wards."

None of his business. Noted. Change of subject.

Abigail pulled him into the cool air of the feed store, and the old wood floors creaked. Hay, fresh sawdust and leather hit his senses. If he had a home, it would smell like this.

As a kid, his favorite place was the stables. On the worst days of Juan Carlos's temper, he would hide in the tack room. He swallowed a lump. He was being ridiculous. As a grown man, the smell of feed and livestock should not make him emotional.

He needed sleep. He focused on Abigail and entered a strange but comforting world.

She took him through the aisles and carefully looked at everything to find the best buy. Why was she being so nice? She had to have an angle, but he couldn't figure it out, not yet.

Maybe she was in a long game to get revenge for her family. He sighed. That sounded a little melodramatic, but after yesterday, who knew?

Abigail stopped in front of a display of leashes and collars. "What color of collar do you want?" Abigail asked. When he didn't answer, she looked over her shoulder.

He was staring at a large refrigerator with glass doors. Hands in pockets, he was scrutinizing the contents. When she stepped close, he looked up at her. "This says it's a healthier choice for digestion and coat. Little Momma's coat needs all the help it can get."

Leaning in, she saw the prices. "For that small bag of food? And it has to be refrigerated? You know in the wild they eat dead things, right?"

"Hey, Abigail." Thalia, Fernando's granddaughter, gave her a quick hug. "What brings you into the store today?" Her gaze cut to Kingston, and she smiled. He smiled back.

An unfamiliar and ugly emotion hit Abigail without warning. Was she jealous? She had never been jealous one day in her life. Even when clients had flirted with her ex-husband, Daniel, she knew it didn't mean anything. As it turned out, she should have been more concerned.

For her, trust was the foundation of a solid marriage. He hadn't even cared enough to apologize when she caught them. But that was the past. He wasn't her problem anymore.

So why the ugly twist in her gut over these two sharing a smile? She narrowed her eyes at Kingston. Maybe because she couldn't have him? But she didn't want him. She didn't.

He was too…everything. She wanted simple and steady. Not that she wanted anything at all.

She blew out a puff of air. He had all her thoughts upside down. She wasn't interested in dating anyone. She wasn't.

"So, who is your guest?"

Right. "Thalia, this is Kingston Zayas. He needs some good work jeans, a few comfortable shirts and—" she lifted her basket of pet supplies "—all the things for a tiny dog and kitten."

She looked at Abigail with a light in her eyes. "Is this the cowboy who had the showdown at church with your grandfather? Heard you stared down Old Man DeLeon. Not a feat for the weak of heart. So, what type of dog? And, aw. You have a kitten, too?" She moved in and placed a hand on his arm.

"They came as a package deal. A very unlikely duo, origins unknown."

Was it her imagination or had he stepped closer to her and away from Thalia? His arm brushed hers. It had to be an accident.

"You rescued them? My poor heart can't take it." Thalia put a hand on her chest. "Will you be in town long?"

Thalia's dark eyes looked at Kingston as if he were the sun and she was Icarus. Thalia was a beautiful woman. And she loved to flirt.

"No."

"Here." Not wanting to watch anymore, Abigail thrust the basket at him and forced a smile. "Thalia can help you with all the rest. I need to head over to the courthouse before they go to lunch. I'll meet you at The Nest. Thalia, if you would pack everything up, Cindy will be by to pick it up and take it out to Tres Amigos."

"Not a problem."

Abigail left without waiting to hear anything else. Thalia was beautiful, single and didn't have kids. She was also a lot of fun. If Kingston was looking for someone to hang out with, Thalia would be perfect.

Jogging across Main, she made her way to the courthouse. Thanks to the tip she had received after the wedding, she was able to pay the ticket off sooner than expected. It was a huge weight off her shoulders.

Afterward, she killed some time visiting with June. She'd worked in the county offices as long as Abigail could remember. The older woman had gone to school with her parents and had helped out her family after the car accident. June was the only female her grandfather had let come in the house—and that hadn't been often. He said no one could replace his wife or daughter-in-law. Abigail hadn't wanted them to be replaced, but being the only girl was lonely.

Bella Zapata walked in. "Abigail." She drew out her name. "I hear you're walking around town with that good-looking, sharp-dressed boy. Does that mean he's worth enduring the wrath of the DeLeon men?" With a wink, she went behind the counter. "He must be something if you're willing to risk all that."

"What's this? You have a beau?" June shook her head. "You were always drawn to those sharp-dressed city boys."

Bella gave her the side-eye and nodded. "To make matters worse, he's a Zayas."

June gasped. "Girl, are you trying to give your grandpa a heart attack?"

"It's not like that." She wanted to bang her head against the limestone wall. It was like that, but she wasn't going to act on it. "Yes. He's a Zayas. I work for them, remember?"

"I hear Juan Carlos is forcing them to live on the ranch together for five years before they can inherit a dime. Mean old coot. If they don't, it's all going to his other kids. He has like six or seven and didn't leave them anything."

"No. Naomi has two half siblings and I think they have the properties in Dallas. And it's only a year. Not that it's any of our business. You both should know better than to believe anything you hear in town."

"All I know is outsiders are buying up everything they can. Another twenty years and there ain't going to be any family ranches left." June grimaced at Abigail. "Sorry. But at one time, not so long ago, your family had the largest ranch in the area. Now look at you. Working for the Tres Amigos Ranch and Resort. What a silly name."

Would she always have to defend her bosses? "The ladies at Tres Amigos are wonderful. It's a great job and I'm focused on raising my son right now. It's been great, ladies, but I've gotta go."

With a wave, she went out the door and walked up the hill to the café. Kingston was not her type, not anymore. She'd learned her lesson, right?

At the top of the hill, standing in front of The Nest, was a newly dressed Kingston. He had a pair of perfectly fitted jeans, a light blue shirt and boots. He must have gone back to Carter's for them.

A smile softened Kingston's face when he spotted her. Her stupid heart hiccupped. *Nope. None of that.*

"Abigail!" He greeted her. "Look who I ran into."

A man stood next to a black dually truck and matching gooseneck horse trailer. How had she missed seeing him?

"Mike Davis. He's the new wrangler. Even came with trail horses ready to ride. This is Abigail DeLeon...uh, Harris. She's the event coordinator on the ranch."

"Well, howdy, Miss DeLeon uh Harris." He winked at her. "No one told me such a pretty gal would be running the events. I would've gotten to Texas a lot sooner." Mike was somewhere in his mid- to late-thirties. He had the perfect Hollywood cowboy look. The guests were going to love him.

She gave him a polite smile and shook his hand. "Just DeLeon is fine. Where are you coming from?"

"Been working big ranches in Montana and Wyoming, but my last gig was in Canada. Looking to get some warmer weather."

"You're in the right place then." She pulled her hand free. Her gut told her that small talk and tall tales were all she would get from the new wrangler, but it would be rude to leave him standing alone in the parking lot. "Mr. Zayas and I were about to eat lunch. Do you want to join us?"

"That's mighty kind of you, ma'am." Mike tipped his hat and grinned at her.

She wanted to tell him to cut the gentlemanly cowboy act with her, but she should give him a chance. Maybe he was just being himself. Kingston gave her a look she couldn't read.

Kingston might not be a real cowboy, but he never pretended to be one either. She sat in her favorite booth and Kingston slid in next to her, forcing Mike to sit opposite them. A few of the locals greeted her and she introduced the men.

More than a few curious glances followed them. Great. By tomorrow morning, rumors would have her in some love triangle with the two strangers in town.

She was more like a square and was very happy staying in her box, alone. Kingston's hand brushed hers as he picked up a menu. Her box was just the right size for her and Leo. No room for anyone else. Nope. She had the lid locked down tight.

Chapter Eight

Abigail called Cindy to let her know they had a ride with the new wrangler. Kingston offered to help unload horses. With each horse he took time to introduce himself before he unloaded them from the trailer. He casually checked for any clues of injury or stress.

She had seen her twin, Isaac, do this a hundred times. He said horses had blind spots and counted on the handler to set the tone and make them feel safe.

With both men stalling the newcomers, she backed the last gelding out of the trailer. Staying close, she rubbed her hand down the neck and over the shoulder. None of the horses had worn any protective wear on their legs. Her brothers always used shipping boots or at least wrapped the horses' legs when transporting them.

This one's leg was hurt. Walking the horse to the last stall, she called Mike over. "This boy has a cut on his heel bulb and his fetlock looks swollen. I'm sure they have a first aid kit in the tack room. Want me to do it?"

Kingston came over and stood close to the horse while inspecting the injury. "He's going to need rest. No one is riding him for a while."

"Idiot horse fought the trailer. I'll take care of the leg." Mike left for the tack room.

Kingston checked the horse. The gelding's head was low. "I'm kind of worried about a couple of them. They don't look alert."

She leaned in and lowered her voice. "You think they're drugged? And why aren't their legs wrapped? Do you wrap yours when you trailer them?"

"Always. We train them for it."

"Found it." Mike came out with a large orange tack box. "Looks like there's everything I need. I'll take care of him. Thanks for the help."

"Not a problem. Where are they from?" she asked.

"I swung by the Childress place on my way down."

She studied the horses. "These are Childress stock?" That surprised her.

He shrugged. "Haven't looked at their papers yet. You know them?" His jaw was doing double time on his wad of gum.

"Two of my brothers work with them." Why was she being so judgy? Tyler Childress could have picked them up at an auction to save them. It was the kind of thing he'd do. She smiled. "We'll let you get to the horses. See you later."

Kingston nodded and followed her out the double doors. "I'm going to check on Fuego. Want to meet him?"

She nodded and they fell into step.

The large pen had a pole shed with a feed and water trough. Two large oak trees were at the corner giving plenty of shade. They approached the railing and Kingston pulled an alfalfa cube from his pocket.

At the far end of the pasture, a striking red stallion lifted his head. He snorted, challenging Kingston, then shook his head as if dismissing him. But the horse's ears flicked as he trotted along the railing. "Is he pretending to ignore you?"

He chuckled. "Yes. I have to earn his attention. Hey, boy.

It's all yours. Come get it." Kingston climbed the railing and jumped to the ground. He held the small cube of compressed green hay out to the horse.

Fuego tossed his head, then spun away from them along the opposite fence line. "Oh, he's showing off for you." Kingston eyes shone with pride. "He's a beauty, isn't he?"

The bloodred horse pivoted off the railings and ran straight for them, his legs eating up the ground. Abigail forgot to breathe. "He's magnificent."

About twenty feet from them, he darted to the left. Running in a big circle, he snorted again and pranced with head and tail held high. He stopped about six feet away from Kingston. The man laughed and held out the treat. "You got to come all the way in, big guy. I have someone for you to meet."

He waved her closer to the railing. The horse's desire for the treat beat out his distrust. Once he accepted the treat, all reservations vanished. Kington rubbed the big horse's forelock and the stallion leaned into him.

Kingston looked up at her. Total joy sparked in his eyes. They stole her breath. She identified with the horse. One step too close and she would lose the fight to stay indifferent.

"He was in Houston as an older yearling. There was a hurricane, and the stables were hit hard. His legs had been injured. His owners at the time thought he would never make it to the track. But no one told him he wasn't supposed to want to race anymore. It's in his heart. His first two races out he won. He loved every minute of the competition." He rubbed under the big jaw. "The barn fire messed with him mentally, but with a little TLC he'll be back."

"So, you love an underdog?" She climbed on the midrail and leaned over the fence. Kingston handed her an alfalfa cube. Laying it flat on the palm of her hand, she offered it to the stallion. With one sniff, Fuego nudged her, then picked up the cube with his lips. She laughed at the tickling sensation.

"Doesn't everyone? Plus, I've been at the losing end one too many times in my life." He grew serious and he caressed the horse's neck. "When I saw the flames consuming the barn, all I could think of was I had put these beautiful animals in danger. I was supposed to take care of them, and I didn't."

"It wasn't your fault, was it?"

"There had been a grass fire at our neighbor's that got out of control."

"That must have been a horrible sight, but accidents happen. We want to find a reason. To blame someone, even if it's ourselves."

For a long moment, he stared over the horse's withers. "Is that why your grandfather blames my mother for the car accident?"

"Wow. You went there." Her gaze fell.

He blew out a puff of air and said something in Fuego's ear, then patted the horse. "Want to go visit Little Momma and Baby?"

She was relieved he didn't push for an answer. "More underdogs you've given a home to. Lead the way."

Kingston went through the gate this time and waited for her. Taking a deep breath, she tried to get past the giddy grasshoppers low in her tummy.

The deep porch of the old bunkhouse gave them a break from the sun. As soon as he opened the door, little paws pattered across the old wood floor. He went down on one knee and the odd little duo showered him with love.

After greeting Kingston, the little dog came over to

make sure Abigail meant no harm. Picking the pup up, she brought her to eye level. The pink tongue gave her excited kisses. The stubbed tail wagged the whole bottom half of Little Momma. "They make a person feel very appreciated."

Going to the small refrigerator, he pulled out the expensive food and put the kitten down. Little Momma wiggled free and went straight to her bowl.

Then he came over to Abigail, gazing at her hair. "You have an oak leaf," he said softly, reaching for it. He paused. Their eyes locked.

Time froze as all of her senses went on alert. He was going to kiss her, and she was going to kiss him back.

Leaning closer, they were a mere butterfly wing apart. She closed her eyes, waiting for contact.

"Abigail?" His low guttural whisper fluttered over her skin.

She nodded, giving permission.

"Abigail! Kingston?" His mother's voice broke the silence like a shot gun.

They jumped apart and turned to the door.

"There you are." Her smile faltered as her gaze bounced between them. "Did I interrupt something?"

"No, no." He rubbed the back of his neck and kept his focus fixed on the cat and dog. "We had… Then the…" A hand waved toward the pair now eating. "Um. I checked on Fuego and then wanted to show her…them."

Apparently, she had recovered faster than him. "Letti, were you looking for me?"

Her gaze left her son and focused on Abigail. The pinched forehead indicated she wasn't happy. "Your grandfather called the office looking for you. Leo fell from his horse. He said you needed to come home as quickly as possible."

All the blood left her body. "To the house? Not a hospital?"

She nodded.

"Thanks." She grabbed the oversize purse she had dropped when the little dog had leaped on her.

Her son was hurt and needed her. What was she doing? Acting like a teenager whose crush talked to her for the first time. She started praying and ran out before she realized she didn't have a car.

Naomi pulled up in one of the ranch trucks. "Letti said you'd need a ride."

"Thank you." She climbed in and continued praying, asking for forgiveness for being distracted. She didn't look back. Her life, her heart, was hurt on her family ranch.

She had no business even thinking that Kingston could be a part of that life.

Kingston went to the door. He needed to go with Abigail. Her son was hurt.

His mother stopped him. "Kingston. Where are you going?"

"Abigail might need me. If Leo is being taken to the hospital she can't drive. I can take her."

"No. She has her brothers. Her family will take care of her. She doesn't need you. It will just cause more stress if you go."

He wanted to argue, but she was right. Abigail didn't need him. In her rush, she had left the door open. He moved to close it.

Resting his hand on the door, he saw Naomi's truck leave. There was a reason he had a rule about single moms, and he'd just broken it. That wasn't fair to her or Leo. He knew firsthand how kids could be confused by people coming and going in their lives.

"Kingston, don't." There was a pleading in her voice.

"I'm just closing the door." He rested his palm on the old wood. He needed to close the door to any romantic thoughts of Abigail.

"As soon as Naomi returns, we're sitting down and talking. No holding back." The words were much more confident than her delivery of them. Arms crossed, she rubbed her elbows, then released them. The action was repeated several times. "We need total honesty with each other."

They had been doing so well since he had arrived. It was the first time ever he'd felt like he had a mother with a solid grip on reality. But now they were going to call him out. He was only here because he needed something from them.

Was she going to revert to manipulating him by guilt? She had always fallen into victim mode and ran away when life got too hard for her to handle. She had run from him even when he was a child.

"Really?" All his old defenses exploded out of their box. "Like why you introduce yourself as Letti Zayas when we both know you're legally a DeLeon? Why do they blame our whole family for a car accident that happened in another state?"

Her eyes went wide, and her mouth fell open like she couldn't breathe. Layers of hurt he would never fully understand clouded her eyes.

Great, he was truly a top-notch jerk. Closing his eyes, he rubbed his brow, hating how he sounded like the angry teenager who apparently still lived inside him. He also heard Juan Carlos coming out of his mouth. It was the guilt wrapped up with the unsteady ground he stood on and the unsettling feelings he had for Abigail.

He would have kissed her if his mom hadn't charged in. With a deep inhale, he looked up. Letti's bottom lids were barely holding back tears from falling. Blinking several times, she kept her focus on Baby pushing her bowl, trying to get a last bite of food.

Kingston went to her and pulled her close. "I'm sorry, Mom. I have a long list of things going wrong, but you're not one of them. I love you." How long had it been since he had said those words to her? Had he been holding them back to punish her?

"I'm so sorry," he muttered against her hair.

Tears dampened his shirt, and he pulled her closer. "It's going to be okay." He didn't know if it would, but the words wouldn't hurt.

Finally, she took a deep breath and stepped out of his arms. With the bottom of her T-shirt, she wiped her face. He went to the sink and ran a towel under the water. Handing it to her, he placed the other hand on her shoulder and lowered his chin to make eye contact. "Are you good?"

With a sigh, she nodded. "Better than I have been in my whole life. That was an overreaction. But I'm also worried about you and Abigail. I like her, but with our families' painful history it's too complicated. You don't need that. Leo and Abigail don't need that."

He was about to protest that nothing was going on between him and the event coordinator, but there had been enough lies. "I agree. Thank you for the reminder."

She creased her brow. "That was easy."

"It was honest. I hope we can start from a place of truth. I do love you." Taking the tea towel from her, he pulled out a chair at the table and invited her to sit.

With a tentative smile, she nodded and sat. After a few minutes of silence, she pulled an envelope out of her bag and put her hand over it. "Naomi and I went to Kerrville this morning. We stopped at the office of Juan Carlos's lawyer. We needed to notify him you were here, so the countdown to the year can officially start."

With a sigh, he planted his elbows on the table and leaned his forehead against his palm.

"That's a good thing," she said, reaching her hand out. He took it.

"No. It's not. I wanted to talk to you together, but I need you to know I don't plan on staying. This ranch doesn't have anything to do with me. My plan was to let you and Naomi inherit the whole thing. I was going to stay out of it and focus on my new venture. Axel and I were just getting our business running, but there was a fire. Our barn and apartment are a total loss. That's why I asked to bring Fuego down here. I need your help."

She squeezed his hand, and he found a depth of concern he wasn't expecting.

"That's devastating, *mijo*. Why didn't you call or say something the minute you arrived? We'll help any way we can."

"Well, that's what I want to talk about." Tires crunched the gravel on the drive outside. The engine cut off and a door slammed shut.

She stood, relief on her face. "Naomi."

He didn't remember the two women being this close before. Naomi had seemed to avoid them his whole life.

His mother rushed to the door and had it opened before Naomi could get in. She grabbed the younger woman's hand and pulled her to the table. "Kingston's barn and apartment were destroyed in a fire. He was afraid to tell us. I reassured him that we'll help." She glanced at him. "Do you need a place for the rest of your horses? You can set up training here if you want."

The two women sat across from him. He went over all the details of the fire and insurance. The plans he and Axel had made and the shortfall of cash. "That's where you come in. I was hoping you would be able to buy me out, or I could take a line of credit against my portion of the ranch. What do you think?"

They looked at each other. Letti bit her bottom lip and glanced at Naomi. "Inheritance of the ranch is pending. Starting as soon as the three of us are living here together for a year. We can't use the ranch to help you other than offer you a place for you and your horses. Axel too."

"What happens if I leave and don't stay?" he asked.

Naomi's shoulders dropped. "Two years from his death, the ranch goes back into the estate, which includes my half siblings, Sydney and Mateo. For now, they have the properties in Dallas. But if we don't meet the stipulation then the ranch will be sold and divided between us. The ranch is the most valuable asset in his estate, so Sydney and Mateo would be happy. If we don't stay you would get a portion of that inheritance, and you could use it however you want. But it will take a few years to get it. It wouldn't help your situation now. I'm sorry." She was sincere.

"It's okay. Axel and I are looking into other options. This was just the fastest." He sat back and watched Little Momma groom Baby. The purrs were loud. "So, with the ranch, what happens? I can't leave for a year?"

"You're not a prisoner," Letti said. "For the next year, it must be your home base, with you involved in the running of the ranch. You can go to Dallas for business trips when needed. Moving your operation here even temporarily could work."

He sighed. "I don't know. Our connections are in Dallas. I'll have to talk to Axel."

They shared another loaded glance. With a deep breath, Letti turned to him. "There is something else we need to talk about that might push you one way or another. It's the reason my brother wanted to force us to work the ranch together for a year." She slid the envelope across the table to him.

"What's this?" His instincts warned him not to pick it up.

"When we went to the lawyer's office, he gave us three letters. My brother wrote one for each of us and it explains why he had this stipulation."

"Do you know what it says?" He eyed the nondescript white paper.

"We haven't read yours, but I'm sure it's basically the same as ours. I don't know how to say this. It should have never been a secret."

His core tightened. "Is it about me?"

They both looked tortured. He sat up. "How much worse is it? Just say it."

Letti took a deep breath and grabbed Naomi's hand. "I'm not your birth mother. Naomi is."

His vision blurred. "What?"

Naomi glanced at Letti, then him. "I was still in high school, and my father was very traditional. Letti had just lost her baby and was in a deep depression that went untreated. He thought if he gave her my baby to raise it would fix everything."

He just stared at them.

"You've asked about your father before. When you thought... Well, I have his name and information if you want it. The last day I saw him was in Juan Carlos's study. Our plan was to tell Father and stand up to him. We were going to run away if he wouldn't support us."

She looked down and steadied her breathing. "Of course, he didn't support us. At first he was so calm. Then he pulled out his checkbook and offered Mac a ridiculous sum of money to sign over his rights and disappear. I thought Mac would tell him that I was worth more than all his money. But there was this long heavy silence." She swallowed. "He didn't even look at me as he took my father's money. He muttered sorry as he went out the door. Father made sure that was my last contact with him.

"I thought he was the love of my life, but then again, I was only sixteen. Father wanted to make sure I knew the truth. People couldn't be trusted. He said a baby would destroy the future he had planned for me. And his sister needed something to replace what she had lost."

He blinked. It was a horrifying story. A story that didn't feel like his. Thinking of the heartbreak a teenage girl had to have gone through, pregnant and alone. A woman who had just lost her husband and baby. So much of his childhood made sense now. He looked at his mother.

"Did you even want me?"

Her mouth opened and closed. "I…"

Apparently, she didn't have an answer to that question. Which was an answer. He stood, not knowing what to do with the raw energy surging through his body.

His mother, Letti, stood too.

"Do I still call you Mother?"

"I'm still your mother." She flattened her hand over her heart and clenched it. "I wasn't the best and I made so many mistakes, but I have always loved you." She looked at Naomi and reached out to her. The women joined hands. "We both loved you. From the first time we heard your heartbeat. Neither of us were in a place to tell my brother no."

Naomi had tears in her eyes. "I didn't know what to do.

I didn't have my mother and Letti was the closest thing I had to a mom. With Letti caring for you, you would stay in my life. We wanted to be open about it, but Juan Carlos wouldn't hear of it. We didn't have any other family and Father moved me to a private high school in another state. Letti went with me. She had an apartment and made sure I went to all my doctor appointments."

Letti said, "I really tried my best to be what my brother wanted from me and be a mother to you. I had promised Naomi that I'd take care of you, but my…" Naomi pulled her close.

"It's okay. Father refused to acknowledge that there was anything such as mental illness. He told us we just needed to be stronger. I had a hard time being around you as a baby." Her tears fell freely now. "I just wanted to grab you and run. But where would I go? Letti was my support during that year. So as soon as I graduated from high school I went as far as I could for college and didn't return home for years." She pulled Letti's head to her lips. "I'm so sorry I wasn't there for either of you."

The understanding of who he was had shifted so fast he couldn't keep his balance. Letti looked down. "I should have been stronger and reached out to you for help."

Naomi kept a tight grip on his mother's hand. This secret had been theirs for almost thirty years. They had a bond that he was not a part of.

"Can you forgive us?" Naomi reached out, but he moved away from them.

"I don't think it's a matter of forgiveness." He tried to put words to his feelings. If there were any, he didn't know them. "I need time to sort through this."

"Of course," they said in stereo.

To say Juan Carlos was controlling was like saying a

sloth was slow. Naomi had moved as far away as possible for college. Letti had followed jobs and boyfriends. Kingston had basically moved in with Axel's family. They had all tried to find a way to escape Juan Carlos's dominating personality. And now, even dead, he tried to control them.

He glanced at the envelope on the table.

Following his gaze, Naomi went to the table and picked it up. "I regret many things, but the biggest is taking the coward's way out to avoid my father. I wasn't there for you or Letti when you needed me. I'm sorry."

Holding the letter out to him, she waited for him to take it. "Letti's your mother. I gave up that right, then lost it when I ran. You don't ever have to accept me even as family if you don't want to." Her voice betrayed the deep emotions she was trying to bury. "But read this. We will be waiting for your decision. Whatever you feel it needs to be. We both want the best for you."

Letti stepped closer, but didn't reach for him. "We had a plan to convince you to stay here and work with us, but we've decided no more manipulation. Read the letter then decide what's best for you. We'll accept your choice. And if there's any way we can help you and Axel, we'll do it."

Naomi's hand started to tremble. He shook the fog out of his head and took it.

Lifting his gaze, he looked at them for a minute. "I need time. This has been…a lot."

"Take all the time you need," Letti said eagerly.

"Well, not all the time." Naomi's voice was hesitant. "We kind of need to know what direction we're going with the ranch. But a week? Would that be good?"

"I think so. If I need more time, I'll let you know."

"I've made a pot roast. It'll be ready in a couple of hours.

Do you want to join us for dinner?" He hated the hopeful edge of Letti's voice because he was going to stomp it out.

"Not tonight."

After several seconds of awkward silence that seemed more like hours, they left.

He looked at the letter. If he had a fire going, he'd toss it in the flames. Grabbing his hat, he went out the door.

He passed through the stable to his red flame in the pasture. It didn't take long to have Fuego saddled and ready. Once out of the barn area, he realized he had no clue where to go. They rode across the pasture until they came to a line of cedar. The sound of water was on the other side. It must be the Frio River.

He dismounted then led the horse along a narrow path through the trees. On the other side was a small grassy area that had a huge rock ledge overlooking the river. Below him swam the most intriguing woman he had ever met. She went under the water then resurfaced and swam to a bright green kayak.

Abigail DeLeon was the distraction he needed.

Chapter Nine

Abigail was furious with her grandfather. Her son *had* fallen off his pony, but there was no injury. Leo had gotten right back in the saddle and was excited to tell her how he had helped find three calves.

Her grandfather had gone out of his way to make her believe Leo was hurt, then accused her of not being a good mother because she allowed a Zayas to distract her.

Not wanting to be treated like a child, she'd started yelling. Not the best way to prove her maturity. Her family pushed her buttons the way no one else could.

Isaac had suggested taking Leo and the kayaks to the river. He knew the Frio always calmed her and he hated it when she was agitated. They had come to Leo's favorite swimming hole. Giant cypress trees towered over her, creating a canopy.

She floated on her back and studied the movement of the branches and clouds above her. The sun found its way through the trees and warmed her face.

She took a deep breath and went under the cool water. Isaac had offered to take Leo back to the house when her son had grown bored and hungry. In a rush to get away from her grandfather, she had forgotten to pack snacks. Maybe she did need to step it up as a mother.

She went under one more time then swam to her kayak. The almost kiss with Kingston had thrown her off-kilter.

Bless her twin for giving her a few minutes alone to re-center. There would be no more thoughts of kissing Kingston. No Kingston period. It didn't matter how energized she was around him. Tension with her family was enough reason to stay away from the man.

Swimming across the river to her kayak, she forced her thoughts into other areas. Time to start dinner.

A movement behind her caused her to turn. She blinked. "Kingston?"

Had her mind conjured him just to prove how futile it was to think she could block him from her mind? No. He was real. He and Fuego stood on the huge rock ledge that hung out over the river.

He gave her a half-hearted smile. "I just needed some time alone. Wasn't expecting a river nymph."

"What are you doing roaming the ranch without an escort? Are you lost?" Something was off.

"Are we on your property?" He dropped the reins in the grassy area behind him then came down the slope to the rocky riverbank. There was an air of defeat around him, like life was just too much to handle. She had seen that in her brothers.

"You're still on your ranch, but the river is public." She pulled herself up into the kayak. "This is the deepest swimming hole in our area. Leo and Isaac just left."

•"Since you're playing in the river, I figured your little man was okay. What happened? Your grandfather made it sound life-threatening."

He sat down.

She used the paddle to hold the kayak in place. "My grandfather was being a jerk. He overreacted when he heard

I spent the morning with you. As soon as I stepped through the door, Leo bragged about his adventure, then went upstairs. Tito gave me a lecture." She lowered her voice to sound like a grumpy old man. "'You should have been home like a good mother. Instead, you're running around town with that Zayas boy. Then, on your day off, you spend time on that ranch.'" She sighed. "I might have raised my voice. It upsets Isaac when we yell. So, he brought me and Leo here. We wash off the dirt of the day and start fresh."

"The river makes a bad day better?" He pulled one boot and sock off then the other. An envelope went from his jeans to a boot.

"What are you doing?" She paddled backward to put more distance between them.

With bare feet, he climbed on a large tree root. "Getting a fresh start. I've never been in the Frio. Is it as cold as the name implies?"

"You'll get your clothes wet! Jeans are the wors—"

He jumped in before she could finish the words. He resurfaced with a yell. "Cold!"

Laughing, she paddled around him. "I warned you. Now you're going to be stuck in wet jeans until you get home." *Home.* Where did he consider home?

He pushed his wet hair out of his face then floated on his back. "It's a shock to the system, but a good one. Sorry to cause a fight with your grandfather. Grandfathers seem to be causing all sorts of trouble today." He went under, then came up for air close to the roots. Just using his arms, he pulled himself up and out of the water.

Turning, he sat on the root and wiped the water off his face.

"Grandfathers? You're having grandfather issues?" He had never mentioned one before and Letti's father was dead.

She paddled closer and pushed the tip of her kayak onto the rounded rocks of the shallow edge of the river before tossing him her towel.

"Yeah, it was news to me too."

"Well, my grandfather is not your problem. What has yours done to make you hazard the wilds alone and using the Frio for shock therapy?"

She should be leaving, not asking questions about his personal life. But she knew how overwhelming the world could be and being alone was the worst.

Tilting his head, Kingston studied her. "You aren't wearing any of your colorful glasses. I've never seen you without them."

"I don't wear them in the water. I have contacts."

He nodded and picked through the rocks and found what he was looking for, then skipped it across the water. "I like your glasses. They're a clue to your mood."

"Really?" A fluttering low in her tummy made her want to giggle. *No.* She should be uncomfortable that he knew her so well. "I just pick the ones that feel right for the day."

He grunted as if that proved his point then skipped another rock.

"That was a good one." She turned to him. "Just so you know, I can spot a first-rate avoidance scheme. I grew up with five pros."

She pushed herself out of the kayak and sat on a large rock. Close, but not too close. "Kingston, what's going on?"

"Other than my dreams of breeding and racing horses going up in smoke? Literally. Today, I was told my uncle is my grandfather and my cousin is my mother. Juan Carlos set this whole thing up, so we're forced to spend a year together."

"Your birth mother is Naomi?" She wasn't as shocked

as she should be. She'd noticed so many similarities between them.

He skipped another rock, but she didn't count this time. She searched his face for clues. "How do you feel about that?"

"I'm great." A dry, sarcastic laugh said otherwise. "That's why I got on a horse and rode until I was lost." There was a long pause as he studied the landscape. She was sure he wasn't seeing the hills or water.

He sighed and lowered his gaze. "Juan Carlos made them keep it a secret during his life. Then he used his death to force us together after years of pushing us apart. I spent half my life trying to get out from under his control."

"What is it about grandfathers? I love mine dearly, but he can't let go of shaping how he thinks my life should be." She wished she had some way to make him feel better, but there was nothing else to say.

He pulled a folded envelope from one of his boots. "He left us each a letter to be given once all three of us were on the ranch. Is it wrong that I just want to chuck it into the river and not let him have the final word?" He stared at the white paper.

"That's justifiable. But if you do, your mind will keep wondering what he said, and you'll have no way to answer that question."

She shifted on the rock so she could rest her hand on his arm. Her instinct was to climb up on the root and put her arm around him, but she still had enough sense to keep space between them. "You could put it away until you're ready."

With a lopsided grin, he handed her the envelope. "Or you could read it. Then give me a summary. He's not talking to me so he can't have the last word."

Opening the letter, she scanned the writing. "It's handwritten." She glanced at him. "You sure you want me to read it?"

Flipping a flat rock in his hand, he shook his head. "He had cancer for a year, but didn't tell any of us. He was so stubborn and didn't want to appear weak. Why couldn't he just talk to us?" Anger pitched his voice. "Instead, he had to be all dramatic and deliver a will stipulation and letters from the grave. Just once I would have liked an honest conversation with him. But no. He had to always be in control."

With an angry thrust of his arm, he flung another rock across the river's surface. "I'm not going to let you control our last conversation," he yelled to the sky. "My mom needed real help, not a newborn, to help her cope with everything she'd lost. Naomi needed your support, not lectures on how she had ruined the family's name. No one cares about the family name but you!"

He dropped his head. The sounds of the river and trees mingled with his heavy breathing. She couldn't sit so far away while he hurt. She scooted up along the tree root and put an arm around him. He turned to her shoulder and cried.

Her heart broke. "Juan Carlos wanted to keep his family close and safe, but in his attempts to do what he thought was right, he pushed y'all away, leaving you each isolated and lost."

He lifted his head, jaw flexing. "Sorry," he said between clenched teeth.

"No. Don't be. Family is so complicated—mixed with love, expectations and disappointment. My grandfather has some of the same tendencies, but I have three older brothers who play interference. We love him, but as a team he can't control us the way he wants. Letti and Naomi didn't have an opportunity to build that. Juan Carlos hurt y'all in his attempts to help you."

"Your family seems close." His gaze stayed fixed on the water.

"We are, but we have our arguments. Hence me floating in the Frio. But when I get home, we'll talk. Well, I will. I tend to force my brothers to talk about feelings they would rather ignore."

"Like you just did with me?"

"Maybe." She laughed. "My grandfather is a whole other ball of wax. But I think about everything he's gone through in his life, the joys and the devastating losses. He would have liked more control over us, but Cyrus wouldn't let him have it. Thanks to my oldest brother, we each left and came back when we were ready. Then there's our faith. Knowing our trust is in God makes us stronger."

"Growing up, there wasn't as much talk about faith as there was about punishment if you did wrong. My uncle—" he sighed "—my *grandfather* believed in a jealous, vengeful God."

"My faith has been the cornerstone to my life. I always knew if God had me, everything would be okay. Sometimes, I'm impatient and try to change course or jump ahead, but it always comes back to sitting still and listening to Him. It's what I was doing when you arrived."

"That works?"

"I was so mad at my grandfather for using my son to try and control me. In prayer, God reminded me of what was important. We're not perfect, but one of us is always there to help the others. My grandfather views life through a lens of loss. He lost his wife, both sons and a daughter-in-law. He was misguided in his attempt to keep me safe, but it was out of love and fear of me being hurt. It helps when

I focus on the intent. I'll tell my grandfather to never do that again and hopefully he'll listen. But at the end of the day, we know we love each other."

He sighed. "Juan Carlos should have given us the opportunity to talk about it before he died."

"What about Letti and Naomi? How are they taking all this?"

"Not sure." He twisted his lips. "I was kind of caught up in the whole you're-not-my-cousin-you're-my-mom thing to really consider that. From what I got, Naomi didn't want to give me up and Letti hadn't really wanted to take me. But Juan Carlos didn't care. He didn't allow Letti to grieve the loss of her husband or their baby." He blew out a breath of air and dropped his head.

"I've been around them enough to know they both love you. All they talked about when I was first hired was ways to get you to come down. I don't think it was because of the will. They really wanted you here. Then when you showed up, they were giddy, but something else was there. Now I think it was worry. They knew they had to tell you but feared your reaction. They don't want to lose you."

He nodded. "That makes sense. They had to keep this secret their whole lives, but it's new to me." He sighed.

"Do you want me to read it? It's not long." She moved to the rock. Space was good.

"I think they want me to read it, so let's do this for them. Read it out loud." One knee up, he rested his arm across it and looked up to the sky.

Why did their family history have to be so messy? If he ever thought of staying in Rio Bella, she could see herself falling for him. But he wasn't, so she couldn't. And she wasn't sure her grandfather could handle her loving Kingston.

* * *

Kingston closed his eyes and prayed. He prayed for God to open his heart to the words that might bring peace to the two women who loved him. That was something he knew without a doubt. No matter what happened to the ranch, they loved him. Even if he wasn't sure he deserved it.

Abigail adjusted the paper. "'To my grandson. Yes. You have always been my grandson from the minute you were born.'" He could hear Juan Carlos in the words. "'You are the next generation in a proud family. Our roots will always be in Cuba. Your grandmother, Franny, and I met in Cuba. The land of our fathers flows in your blood.'"

She paused. "Um. It's not what I was expecting."

He chuckled. "This is classic Juan Carlos. The part about Franny is new. She's Naomi's mother. But he took every opportunity to remind me we are proud Cubans." Maybe that was all this letter was. One last reminder of his ancestry.

"'I wish I would have been brave enough to call you grandson while I was still breathing.'" She paused and looked at him. "That changed the tone. If you want me to pause or reread anything so you can process it, let me know."

He nodded and swallowed the lump that had formed in his throat. "Go ahead."

"'I wasn't able to help my sister after the loss of that DeLeon troublemaker. He was more than ten years older than her, and I had forbidden her to see him. But she hadn't listened, and vowed she loved him. So, I tried to help and gave him money to pay off a loan shark. That only made it worse. She refused to see the scoundrel he was. When she reached out to his family after he died, they rejected her. I was furious. In her distress, she lost a baby and herself. At her protest, I made her come to Dallas, but I still didn't have my sister. She was a shell of herself. When my daughter came to me and told me she was pregnant, I knew I had failed to protect them both.'"

Abigail paused. He turned to see what had caused it. There were unshed tears in her eyes. "This is when my parents and grandmother were killed in the accident. They had gone to Reno to get Uncle Diego out of jail. I didn't know your grandfather was trying to help him. He must have been desperate after he lost everything. I love Tito, but he was hard on his sons. They say my grandfather swore he'd let Diego rot in jail, which sounds very much like him. But my father and grandmother went to get him. On the way back they think my father fell asleep. Cyrus was in college. Joaquin had a basketball tournament and they dropped me and Isaac off with a friend. My mother and Lucas went with them. He was twelve. Lucas had been sleeping in the back. He was the only one who survived."

She blinked, then looked at him. "I was too young to really remember any of it except the anger and sadness of my grandfather. Isaac was nonverbal and prone to huge fits. We thought it was grief. He was away at college before he was diagnosed with ASD."

"ASD?"

"Autism Spectrum Disorder. He spent his whole childhood and adolescence with us not understanding."

"It's strange how one event shaped us both, and it happened before I was even born."

"So, I'm older than you." Her expression softened, and she almost smiled. He liked that so much better than sadness or worry.

"Not by much." He nudged her shoulder. Reading this letter was too hard on her. "We should stop. It's too personal for you. It seems more about the past than me anyway." It was strange to hear stories that were not part of his memories but affected his family.

"I'm too invested now. It's eye-opening to see another perspective. No one in my family talks about it. I know the bare minimum from people in town, and most of that is probably wrong. This moment in time changed my family. It changed my life."

He studied her face as she found the place where she had left off. Her wet hair had started to dry, curls forming at the ends. Her lashes swept down and out. The golden tone of her dark skin vibrated with energy. Did she see herself as more than just a sister, granddaughter and mom? She was so much more, so captivating.

He closed his eyes to stop himself from looking at her.

"'There was one solution,'" she continued to read. "'Give my daughter's future back to her and give my sister a baby to replace the one she'd lost. You would still be a Zayas, my nephew. I thought I had done the best for everyone, including you. But now that I am forced to sit still and think about the past, I see the mistakes I've made. The three of you have your lives ahead and it should be as a family. My mistakes started in Rio Bella and that is where you'll find the truth of who you are. Please forgive me. All the blame is mine. Letti and Naomi deserved better.'"

Reaching for her, he motioned for her to stop. He heard the words but couldn't process them. "It took him dying to see the hurt he had caused?" Anger swirled in his gut. But guilt too. Did he have a right to be angry at an old man? At two women who had gone along with the lie? Naomi had been a teen, but his mom had been in her early thirties.

He threw another flat rock and watched it skip to the opposite riverbank. Was he ever going to be able to land and find his place in life? He rubbed his neck, then nodded to Abigail to keep reading.

Lowering the paper, her gaze held his. "If you're sad, angry, relieved or guilty, even a mix of them all, that's how you feel. If you allow it to be felt, then you can go through it and move on."

He wasn't sure if that was possible. "Go on."

"'It's too late for me to fix it and I'm a stubborn old man with too much pride to face you. I pray the Tres Amigos brings the three of you together and heals old wounds. Just as I told my sister and my daughter, I will tell you. I love you. Anything I did was from the desire to protect you.'"

She lifted her gaze to his.

"'Your grandfather, Juan Carlos Antonio Zayas.'" After carefully folding the letter, she held it out to him. "It's yours now, and you can do with it whatever you want."

He stared at the paper, not making a move. "Did you know my middle name is Juan Carlos? He wanted a connection with me, but didn't know how."

He finally took the letter and put it in the envelope. He watched the clear water push up against the root he sat on. "Thank you for this. About earlier today, when we almost kissed—"

"I think it's best if we don't even think about it. There's too much at stake for us to enter into a relationship and I don't... Well, I just don't."

"Right." He knew that was the case, so why was he even trying? "Would it be different if I wasn't a Zayas?"

"Or planning to leave soon?" She put her feet in the water. "I don't have the energy to play what-if games."

He wanted to point out that he could change his plans. He could even change his name. But she was right, what-ifs were not fair to her or Leo.

She stood. "Give yourself time before you make any decisions. Once the rawness of the news wears off, you'll have a better understanding of what you want." Stepping into the water, she paused. "When Daniel served me with divorce papers, my world crumbled. I had been willing to forgive his infidelity and move on just to keep our marriage. The word *divorce* terrified me. But he took the choice away and I had to create a new idea of my life and who I was. It's been a little over a year and I'm in a good place. Time and distance help." She pointed to the letter. "It's too new. Turn it over to God."

She got to her kayak and settled in. Her mouth opened as if she had something else to say, but she pressed her lips together and just gave him a nod. Pushing off with her paddle, she made her way upstream against the current.

He watched until she disappeared around a bend.

He needed to call Axel and tell him there would be no financial help coming from the ranch. Maybe he should return to Dallas and beg for his old job back. There was too much to deal with here. He had promised Letti and Naomi he'd stay until the end of the month before deciding what he would do with this information. But at this point, he couldn't imagine remaining here.

Turn it over to God, Abigail had said.

He took a deep breath and looked to the sky.

Chapter Ten

Abigail glanced at her dashboard and resisted the urge to press on the gas. They were five minutes late. She hated being late and she still had to get Leo to the camp registration table.

Having her car back made the week better and she had managed to avoid direct contact with Kingston. She knew Letti and Naomi were worried that he was leaning toward Dallas. But as much as she wanted to ask him how he was doing, she knew keeping her distance was best for both of them.

Work had kept her busy organizing new packages for events, and calling prospective clients and vendors had kept her head down. Naomi and Letti loved the welcome basket idea with the handmade bread and salsa.

Evading Kingston had worked out well too, but the ranch wasn't that big. Was Kingston avoiding *her*?

The unwelcome disappointment had to be shoved aside. There was work to do on Tres Amigos, her family to help and Leo to raise. She was blessed with a full life. Why did the thought of Kingston leaving cloud that?

Potential clients were visiting the ranch today. It would be a big account if they landed it. That had to be her focus.

If Kingston was avoiding her, it was good. *So* good. Everything was fine. She heard her brother Lucas laughing at her. *Liar. Liar.*

She was worried about Kingston. That's all. He'd had earth-shattering news dumped on him, and his barn and apartment were destroyed by flames. She knew all too well what it was like to think life was great, when out of nowhere the ground falls away.

"Mom, will Mr. Kingston be there?" Leo nearly bounced out of his seat belt.

"I don't think you'll see him." *And she was not going to think about him.*

Naomi had allowed the church to host Vacation Bible School at the ranch and Leo was more excited than ever before. She parked the car, and he didn't wait for her to cut the engine before jumping out.

"Leo, wait for me." She swung her purse over her shoulder and stood.

"Mr. Kingston!" her son yelled as he ran to the barn. "You look like a cowboy." The horses standing at the railing turned and ran from the whirlwind rushing toward them.

"Leo." She blew out a puff of air. Sometimes having a son with a little less energy would be nice. There was no point calling him back now. He was already standing with Kingston.

The plan to avoid him was taking a hit, thanks to her son. "Mom, look. Mr. Kingston is a real cowboy." He turned and looked up at his newest hero.

Kingston tipped his Stetson and went down on his haunches to be at her son's eye level. "Even though I'm not an official cowboy, I know we shouldn't run and yell around horses. It spooks them."

Leo nodded. "Sorry. My uncles tell me all the time. I get so excited. My legs turn to bouncy springs." He glanced at the horses. "Are you riding? Can I go?" He finally looked at her.

"You have camp." She gave Kingston a swift glance then looked away and adjusted her glasses. She had picked black today to remind her to stay focused on business. She bit back the urge to tell him they had nothing to do with her mood. "The counselors are forming the groups." She nodded to the other side of the barn where a decorated table was surrounded by kids, teens and a couple of adults.

"But I want to go with Mr. Kingston. I can show him about being a real working cowboy. Tio Lucas says I'm the best."

"You've been looking forward to camp. I think Mr. Kingston can manage one more day without you."

His gaze stayed on Kingston. "Are you sure you don't need me to teach you how to be a real cowboy? The De-Leons are the best."

She pressed her lips together, suppressing a smile. He sounded just like her grandfather. Before she could say anything, Kingston had his hand on Leo's shoulder.

"Hey, partner." He had added a little Texas twang to his voice. It should have been sappy, but he made it sound good. "There's a lot to learn and today is just basically getting the lay of the land. I'll need your help soon."

Leo nodded, then turned his attention to her. "Momma, you're eating lunch with me, right? Can Mr. Kingston join us?"

"I'm sure Mr. Zayas has a busy schedule." She emphasized the *Mr. Zayas* for her son.

Kingston raised a brow. "So formal." He smiled at Leo and stood. "That's a date. I can ask you questions about cattle."

"Yay!" Leo fist-pumped the air. "It's goin' to be lots of

fun. It's a real cowboy cookout just for our first day. Bye."
He gave her a quick hug then ran to join the other kids.

She sighed. It was a blessing that her son made friends
fast. He was the kid who just jumped into a group, and he
would pull others in with him. He was so excited about everything every day. It was exhausting at times.

"It has to be hard raising him by yourself." The deep
voice reminded her she wasn't alone. She closed her eyes
for a second, wishing she had left with her son, but she had
never moved that fast.

"Sorry. Not my business." He stood next to her, watching the kids being sorted. "That is utter chaos."

"It's controlled chaos." She smiled at the sight. "I grew
up being a camp counselor. Those are some of my best
memories."

One of the girls had a clipboard. As she called names,
two of the boys tossed colored bandannas to the kids. Behind them were six other teens with poles, each decorated
with a different color.

She shrugged, still not making eye contact.

"When I first came home after the divorce, I was dev-
astated. It felt like I had failed and was moving backward.
Raising kids was not meant to be done alone, but I have
my brothers and my grandfather. It's been a blessing to
come home to my family. You're right—it's hard, but time
gives you a clearer perspective. If you…" She needed to
stop talking. "Sorry."

He shook his head. "Don't worry about it. Your family
experience is just different than mine." He let out a dry
laugh. "On so many levels. Even before the big reveal, it
was a mess." He sighed. "But when I first arrived, I noticed
my mom seemed to be in a good place. That wasn't the case
growing up, and I was hard on her. Naomi is giving me lots

of space. As in, she's avoiding me. I think she's waiting for me to make the first move." He sighed. "Leo's a good kid. Me? Not so much. I wasn't easy to raise."

"What about your father? Did they tell you anything?"

His lips pulled tight and shook his head. "Naomi said she could give me his information, but he left us for a wad of money. Not sure I care to know him."

"Not even his name or where he's from?" The words were out, and she wanted to pull them back. "Sorry. It's really none of my business."

"I think I just said that to you. His name is Mac and I don't care to know anything else." He gave her a lopsided grin. "You know you're a good mom, right? You put Leo first."

"I try. We all make mistakes. We're human."

Awkward silence fell hard between them. "Well." *Ugh, really?* She pointed to the office down the road. "I have an appointment to show some potential newlyweds and their parents the ranch. I don't want to be late. They're looking for a weekend getaway with one hundred guests next summer. It'll be a big account. The main house should be finished." Why was she still talking? "I'd better go."

She glanced at him. Was he laughing at her? Scowling at him only made it worse. He raised an eyebrow as if to challenge her. They were talking without saying anything. He knew it. She knew it.

"Great. You're both here." Letti came out of the barn. "I came to the horses hoping to find you." She put her hand on Kingston as if he might try to run away.

"I went to the offices first," she said to Abigail. "I was worried. You're never late, but I forgot about the camp."

She took a moment to catch her breath, then looked up at Kingston. "Abigail is meeting with the Barban and Ciceron families in a couple of hours. Camilo and Andrea Barban are old family friends from Cuba. Do you remember them? I think Juan Carlos put you into the same private school their kids went to. I couldn't afford it, but he wanted the best for you. David is the youngest. Did you have classes with him?"

He blinked but she couldn't read his expression. "I did."

Letti bit her lip. "Well, anyway, David is marrying the only child of Phil and Marley Ciceron." She glanced at Abigail. "You've done your research on them, right?"

"Yes. They're high society in Dallas."

Letti turned to Kingston. "If we can convince them to hold the wedding here, they'll book the whole ranch. It would be huge for our cash flow and future bookings. They could help us get fully established as a premier wedding venue. Both families have so much influence." She was practically bouncing with excitement. "Naomi and I were talking and thought it would be very beneficial if you went along. With you and Abigail working together, I know we can secure this booking. They want the whole horseback-on-a-ranch experience for themselves and their guests."

"I had plans to spend the day with Fuego." Again, Abigail couldn't read his tone. Was he happy or upset they were being forced to work together?

Letti hugged him, then stepped back, uncertainty in her eyes. "Sorry. I didn't mean…"

"It's okay," he muttered and gave her a half attempt at a smile.

There was a new fragility around them that hurt Abigail's heart.

"Good. I'll tell Mike to have eight horses ready. The new trail horses were a dent in the account, but now I'm happy we spent the money to ensure we have good ones."

"Since we have a couple of hours, I'm going to visit Fuego." Kingston said.

Letti shook her head. "You should go with Abigail now. She knows the ranch and community better than anyone. If you're still going to upgrade our web page, she can help. Y'all should work together on this."

He glanced at Abigail, who quickly averted her gaze and watched the kids head off to their stations in organized groups.

"Okay." She heard him agree, but he didn't sound happy about it.

"Abigail, I don't know if he told you, but he's an expert on the computer. That was his corporate job before he quit working to go full-time with the racehorses. You both have a good deal of experience and ideas, and this is a great opportunity to bring those together."

Together? Her stomach dropped. From the corner of her eye, she saw him stiffen. It didn't seem he was any happier about this arrangement than she was. She wasn't sure if she should pray for patience or wisdom.

They would be working together. Why did she have the suspicion that God was laughing at her well thought out plans just like her brothers? She was so tired of being laughed at.

He stilled. Letti wanted him to work closely with Abigail. Did she mean to torture him? She was the one who'd lectured him about staying away from the single mother from the DeLeon family.

He glanced at the woman who had been on his mind way too much since he'd arrived. He had been doing so well avoiding her. Abigail had also seen him at his weakest. It didn't sit well with him.

Working with her would be a disaster. But how to get out of it and not be a jerk? He'd have to think of something. But the appointment was two hours away. There was no way he was going to just spend that much time alone with Abigail DeLeon.

"So, you have another appointment?" he asked. "You had said you needed to leave."

Abigail must have found her shoes interesting because her gaze was glued to her feet.

"No," Letti answered, looking confused. "Only one today. I'm going to check on the big house renovation. I really need that to be on schedule. Thanks again for your help."

They were alone. "The meeting is in two hours? I can see why you were in such a hurry to leave."

She glared at him. "I thought we had an unspoken agreement to avoid each other. And what is it with Letti pushing for us to work together?"

He narrowed his eyes as he watched his mother disappear down the path to the hacienda. "I found that a little suspicious. Her last speech about you was to stay out of your life. Now she wants us to work together. I don't get it."

Abigail gasped. "She thinks if we—" she waved her hand between them "—start dating, you'll stay."

"No." He made a face at her. "They said they would respect my decision."

"And I'm sure they will. But they also want you to stay."

He didn't like the thought they would use Abigail. "I'll have a talk with them. If you don't want me to join you for the tour, I can sit it out."

"No. She's right about connections. If the groom-to-be knows you, it can help. Your stallion is past the offices. Let's walk that way. I can show you the packages I'm going to talk to them about. It won't take long so you can go talk to Fuego. I'll text you when they arrive."

They walked past kids doing crafts and another group listening to a story. Leo was in that group and waved to them.

Abigail stopped. Standing next to her, he studied the group of kids around Leo. They each had cut out Popsicle-stick figures that they were using to go along with the story.

"I know it's a touchy subject, but when I walked you home you said we were on land your family owned. That seems to be the biggest point of contention. How did it go from your ranch to our ranch?"

"Cyrus said Tito was hoping Tio Diego would take ranching seriously if he owned a section of land, so he signed a piece over to him. Then Tio died and it all went to Letti since they were married. But no one in my family knew they were married, and it was another shock on top of everything else. Tito accused your mom of tricking Diego. And passed that hatred down to his grandchildren."

He shook his head. "She told me that Juan Carlos had given Diego a large sum of money to pay off his debts. That's the money he gambled away hoping to make more and then tell his family about the marriage. He never knew about the baby."

She sighed. "I wonder if that would have made a difference. He had a gambling and a drinking problem. My grandfather had refused to help him financially. I guess Letti convinced her brother to give him the money."

The whole thing left a heavy weight in his gut. "According to Letti, they had plans of building a house. Then the accident happened, and your grandfather lost his family. I can't imagine the weight of that kind of grief."

She opened her mouth then shut it tight, her eyes wide.

He turned. A burnt orange Suburban passed them and parked in front of the offices.

Getting out of the driver's side, Cindy waved. And she wasn't alone.

"What? Already? Well, so much for having two hours." She grabbed his arm. "I'm not ready. I haven't even showed you the packages." Her breathing was rushed.

"Don't worry. I got this. I'll distract them and you can get ready." Time to be the social creature he had been trained to be.

David crossed the parking lot and slapped him on the back. "I heard you were investing in long shot racehorses, but I find you playing cowboy down here. Have you thought about working with cutting horses? We own a few. We were in Waco looking at adding to our stables. Jay Johnson rides them. We should talk."

"We should. This is Abigail DeLeon. We were lucky to get her from the best Atlanta hotels, but she's also a local so you can't be in better hands if you want the best, most organized ranch experience. Abigail, this is Camilo and Andrea Barban. Their son David."

A tall dark man in his sixties reached out to shake hands with them. "A true pleasure. This is Phil and Marley Ciceron and our future daughter-in-law, Zeta."

There were more smiles and handshakes. Kingston glanced at Abigail. Even though she was smiling and looked happy to greet them, he saw panic in her eyes.

"Abigail has some business to take care of, but I can walk you over to the event barn." He pointed down the path. "We'll come back to the offices and talk details. Then a tour of the ranch on horseback."

Zeta clapped. Her black hair was pulled in a tight ponytail. "That's what I'm most excited about."

David put an arm around her and grinned. "That's why we showed up two hours early. Since we were in Waco it only took us an hour to fly into their little airport here. So quaint. And loved the transportation. Cindy was a wealth of information."

"It was the most unique pickup we have ever experienced. We are looking forward to returning into town for lunch," the bride-to-be's mother added.

"Unique. That's what we want. Right?" Zeta looked up at David.

Kingston nodded to Abigail as the group headed down the path. She mouthed a thank-you to him.

How did she make him feel like a hero for the smallest acts? He could become addicted to her. He followed the Barban and Ciceron families to the barn and glanced at his watch. He could kill twenty minutes for her.

He sighed. If he decided to stay at the ranch, he would love to do a lot more for her, but would she want him to?

Was it too much to ask for one thing, just one, to be simple?

Chapter Eleven

Kingston watched Abigail chat comfortably with the three women as they made their way to the barn. Today, she had simple square black glasses, and her hair was half pulled up. Loose waves bounced around her shoulders as she walked.

When they'd entered her office, her full, bright smile had been on display. He could tell the women were excited about the vision Abigail presented.

Mike met them at the barn doors. "Howdy. I have the horses ready." He tipped his hat to the women. The two older women giggled. *Really?*

Everyone mounted and they followed Abigail. The horses walked in pairs as they passed an old barn that had been renovated as the bridal-party cabin. Abigail took them through a small villa of cottages and then the large hacienda that was under renovation.

"I want to have a real cattle drive experience for our family and friends," Zeta said. "How would that work?"

"We'll have a small herd of cattle in the front pasture and y'all will be able to move them across the river." The horses fell into a single line as they zigzagged up the side of a hill. Kingston rode in the back to make sure everyone stayed safe.

One by one they topped the ridge and gasped. Curiosity

had Kingston standing in his saddle, trying to get a glimpse. He knew from his school days with David that this was a hard group to impress.

He came into the large flat area with a few giant oaks offering shade. He was stunned by the view.

They were on the highest point of the ranch, maybe the county. The valley below held green pastures dotted with cattle and goats surrounded by thickets of trees. The clear blue-green river snaked through the giant cypress trees and around a bend. Layers of hills faded into the horizon. He could see the buildings on Tres Amigos and north of them buildings that had to be part of her family's ranch. Rio Bella was a smattering of buildings in the far distance.

He could own a part of this. No wonder her family was upset about losing any of this land. Images of his race-horses running in the pastures played like a movie. Could they rebuild in the hills of Texas? But they didn't have access to the facilities they needed. And the money it would take. He shook his head to release the fantasy.

Abigail pointed out all the options for the different activities. They asked several questions, and she answered them all with authority and confidence.

She had snacks and drinks in her saddlebag, so they dismounted and enjoyed the view. She talked about having a late-afternoon picnic up here for the first day their guests arrived and watching the sunset.

After more excited conversations, they remounted and headed down the side of the hill.

Kingston scanned the area and checked the horses. The bride's gelding, Dakota, was twitching his ears. They came to another pasture and heard kids' laughter and squeals. Far to their right, groups of camp kids were playing games outside an old barn.

Dakota sidestepped. Zeta was laughing at something David was saying. Kingston eased closer, not liking the way Dakota tossed his head. The horse was agitated, but that didn't make sense. There wasn't an immediate threat, and Mike had reassured him the horses were well trained for trails. Should he stop and suggest they trade horses?

A balloon popped from a game station and kids screamed. All the horses became alert, but Dakota crow-hopped. Zeta screamed and yanked on the reins. The horse reared and Zeta lost her balance, sliding out of the saddle.

Kingston pressed his horse close and caught her, so she landed on her feet, away from Dakota's sharp hooves as he bolted. Abigail was off her horse and at the woman's side in an instant, her phone in hand.

With Zeta safe, Kingston turned to see Dakota running straight to the old barn where the kids had gathered.

"Kingston!" Abigail called and he glanced over. She had seen the same potential disaster he saw. With a nod, he leaned low over his gray and lifted the reins. He had a bad feeling the spooked horse was not going to let the fence slow him down, and kids could get hurt.

Leo was with those kids. Heart in his throat, he pushed his mount harder. He had to stop that horse.

Abigail had called Naomi, and she was on her way with an ATV. "Are you okay?" she asked Zeta.

"Yes." She fixed her hair. "Just embarrassed."

Her fiancé and parents were off their horses and crowding her.

"That horse shouldn't be on this ranch," Marley was yelling at Abigail. "Zeta could have seriously gotten hurt."

"Mom. Please don't. I wasn't paying attention." Zeta

reached for David's hand, and he held it without saying anything.

Abigail nodded. The balloon had been too far away to spook a good trail horse. "I'll make sure he's not used for trail rides again. Naomi is on her way. She can take you to your cabin. Are you sure you don't need us to call an ambulance or to take you to see a doctor?"

"Please, no. I'm fine."

"That horse should be put down. He's an unpredictable menace. Where is the closest hospital?" the mother asked.

"Mom. No."

Abigail wasn't sure if Zeta was arguing for the horse's life or not needing a hospital. So, she ignored the first part. "It's in Kerrville, about an hour's drive."

"Cam!" David's mother yelled. "That mad horse is going to run down the kids!"

Abigail turned her gaze to find Kingston. Her heart slammed against her chest as she watched the scene at the other end of the pasture.

The camp counselors had huddled the children in a tight circle and were herding them to the old barn. The out-of-control horse was charging toward them.

Kingston closed in as they approached the fence. That should stop the horse. She prayed, but before she could finish, Dakota jumped the fence on a direct collision course with Leo's group. Controlling the instinct to yell, so as not to add to the chaos, she watched in horror.

Kingston leaned lower over his horse's neck and moved as one with the large mare. They sailed over the fence on the heels of the runaway. It looked as if Kingston was as good with horses as Letti had said.

He ran alongside the scared gelding and turned his mount's shoulder into the base of Dakota's neck, veering him off his path to the barn. Reaching down, he grabbed the loose reins and kept his mount pressed tight to the scared horse. As a pair, they moved in a large circle.

The loop got smaller until both horses came to a complete stop. He dismounted, checked the gelding's saddle and adjusted the pads. He rubbed the gelding's nose and spoke to him.

After lowering the stirrups, he swung up onto the saddle. Kingston placed a hand on Dakota's shoulder and kept talking as he guided him to the nearby round pen.

He had the split reins of the mare in his free hand, and she stayed close to the gelding. The kids changed course and gathered along the outside of the round pen to watch him create patterns in a slow canter.

"He makes that look easy," Zeta said, breaking Abigail out of her Kingston-induced trance.

"Menace," Marley muttered. "He should be put down."

The sound of the four-wheel utility vehicle had them all turning. "Mrs. Ciceron, the safety of our guests is my number one priority. I promise the horse will be off the trail ride line."

Naomi slowed as she approached them. "I have a first aid kit."

The mother of the soon-to-be bride pointed frantically at her daughter then gestured to the horse Kingston now had under control. "Zeta was thrown from that crazy horse."

Zeta shook her head. "Kingston made sure I landed on my feet away from any trouble. I might have a bruised ego after bragging about my riding skills, but I'm good. I promise." She cut a glance at her mother. "Maybe a long soak in a hot bubble bath."

"I can get you that," Naomi said. "Who wants a ride to the cabin? I can take three."

"The ladies can go with you." David squeezed Zeta's hand. "We'll help Abigail with the rest of the horses."

"Be careful. We don't know if we can trust these horses," Marley said, taking her daughter's hand and settling in the UTV.

Naomi gave a concerned glance to Abigail.

Abigail pointed to where Kingston and the horse were making circles. "One of Mike's new trail horses wasn't as safe as he led us to believe. Kingston has the horse now. I'll talk with Mike."

With a nod, Naomi took off.

As they mounted, her gaze went to Kingston. He had the gelding trotting in figure eights. Leo was sitting on the fence, holding the mare's reins.

Kingston walked the gelding to the fence and said something to Leo. Her son smiled and said something back, then waved his hand in the air. Kingston nodded and backed the gelding up. He turned him in the other direction and galloped in another figure eight.

Her son had the largest smile on his face and Kingston grinned. Her heart did a funny thing, but it wasn't from fear this time.

It should be though. She should be very afraid of the feelings that settled in her gut. Kingston was not an option, not a safe one anyway. And she needed safe. Her son needed a childhood of stability and certainty. He had already had one man walk out on him.

She had a job to do. One of her guests and several children had been in danger today, and a horse had been placed in a situation that wasn't fair to it. Instincts told her Mike had lied. Unacceptable.

They had lost any chance of booking Zeta and David's wedding.

The two men were riding ahead, the horses knowing where the barns were, so she took the time to call her brother. When Mike had told her these were Childress horses, she should have followed her instinct and checked the claim.

Isaac picked up on the second ring. "Abigail. Is everything okay?"

"Yes. Sorry to scare you. But I need some information from the Childress Ranch. Could you check on something for me?"

Chapter Twelve

Kingston eased the gelding into a slow trot. He hadn't wanted to drop the horse off at the stables until he was cooled down and calm. Leaning forward, he patted the sweaty shoulder. "Good boy." The poor horse had been scared out of his mind.

He had seen this before. The horse had trauma in its past and its fight-or-flight response had been triggered. Fighting to keep his anger down, Kingston gave all his attention to Dakota. "You're safe."

At his core, he knew Mike was shady. This poor horse had no business on a trail ride with an unprepared rider. It ate at his core when people misused these beautiful, sensitive animals. He'd seen it in the racing industry, which was why he owned a few of the horses he did, including Fuego.

An audience watched him in the arena as he rode the gelding through controlled patterns. The spectator with the biggest smile sat on the top railing.

"Leo, thanks for holding Sadie. It was a big help."

"You tricked me. You're a real cowboy." The boy was so happy it was infectious.

"There are other types of horse people. What I don't know anything about is cows. I still have a lot to learn there."

"I can't wait to tell Tito what you did today. He says you're up to no good, but that's not true. You saved us and the horse like a good cowboy would." Leo leaned forward to pat Dakota's forehead. The horse closed his eyes and leaned into the touch. "See? He's a good horse. He just got scared."

"You're right about Dakota. Just had a bad experience. No need to tell your grandfather. It'll just upset him. Thanks again for helping, cowboy. I'm going to take these two to the barn and give them some well-deserved treats."

The mare followed close to his side, and he headed to the gate. One of the older counselors opened it for him. As he left the area there was applause. Dakota flicked his ears. Leaning over his neck, Kingston rubbed his hand at the base. "It's okay, boy."

The counselors had hushed the kids and now they had their hands in the air waving silently. He smiled and waved back.

He wasn't sure why, but the sight of the kids silently waving their approval caused a lump to lodge in his throat. Being fully appreciated was a new feeling.

Once he got the horses settled, he would have a word with Mike. If he had his way, the man would be off the property before the sunset.

Raised voices were coming from the barn. Kingston dismounted and led the horses in, not sure what was going on.

Mike yelled it wasn't his fault and that the troubled horse should be put down. The man's face was red, and he jammed a finger in Abigail's direction. Rage tore through Kingston. He was about to charge in and break the dude's fingers. He'd never point at Abigail again.

Rage wasn't a good place to react, so he took a deep breath as he glared at the man and plotted.

Needing to take his gaze off Mike, he checked on Abigail. He stopped and put a calming hand on Dakota, more for himself than the horse.

"It's okay, boy. Look at her. She's got this."

Abigail was standing tall, her arms casually crossed over her chest. Her silent stare should have been a warning to Mike, but the man was too full of himself to see it.

"Are you finished?" she asked. There was a deadly, cold chill to her normally sweet voice as she stood nose to nose with the wrangler.

In that moment, he couldn't deny that he had fallen hard for this woman. She championed the underdog and stood up for what she believed to be right. The term *Mama Bear* was all hers.

"Not the horse's fault. As a wrangler, you have the responsibility to make sure our guests and horses are safe. If you fail at your job, you'll be held accountable."

Mike turned to face someone behind Abigail. Kingston hadn't even noticed Letti standing there. She was shaking her head, looking uncertain.

"Letti." Mike's voice was desperate. "It's not my fault. There was no indication he would do this. He's unpredictable and that makes him dangerous. I agree with Abigail that safety comes first. The fasted cheapest way would be to him put down. We can't sell him. That would risk us getting a bad reputation."

Letti glanced at Abigail and then looked at him. "Kingston? What do you think? Marley Ciceron called me. She's very upset and wants us to take care of the problem."

Before he could respond, Abigail pointed *her* finger at Mike. "He wants to cover his dirty tracks by destroying a perfectly fine horse. He's the problem and I recommend we call the sheriff. This man did go to Tyler Childress, but he tried to sell them horses he had picked up at auction. They said no and sent him on his way. He brought them here and sold them to you."

She was a warrior, and she took his breath away.

"First, he lied about where the horses came from." She held up a finger and started counting off. "Two, he lied about the ranches he worked on. Three, he put a guest and a horse in danger due to his laziness and greed. Four, the receipts he gave you were falsified. He bought all six horses at an auction in Lubbock. Give me a little time and I'll find out what he really bought them for. Letti, I have a feeling he owes you money."

"She's a liar." Mike turned to Letti. "You talked to the ranches where I worked. She's just causing trouble."

Abigail smiled. "Your mistake was claiming they were from the Childress Ranch. The horse world can be small. My brothers work with Tyler and his dad. I'm expecting a call any minute telling us how much Mike bought the horses for."

She finally took her gaze off Mike and glanced at Kingston. "How is Dakota?"

"He's sound. I suspect the balloon popping had him fearing for his life. He's good now, moves well through his gaits. Had him doing flying lead changes with ease. He has a smooth sliding stop. He's well trained and responsive. I would love to know his history. I have experience with these types of horses. My guess is trauma. I wouldn't put him on the trails again but putting him down would be murder. He's a good horse."

Abigail kept eye contact with him, and the rest of the world slipped away. It was just the two of them in the barn. "I promised Mrs. Ciceron I would take care of the problem. I see that in two parts. We need a new wrangler, and I can take Dakota to my brother Isaac. He's a vet and can help us get more information on the horse. What do you think?"

"I agree." He turned to his mother and waited for her response. She was the operations manager.

She nodded. "Abigail, can you take Dakota to your brother now?"

"Sure. I'll get the trailer." She reached out to Dakota and gently rubbed his muzzle.

"I can ride him over across the front pasture. It would be safer than trying to load him."

"Good idea. I'll ride Sadie. She's calm."

Letti stepped in front of Abigail. "I'll call the sheriff. Mr. Davis, please give me your keys." She pointed to Jacob, who stood at the door behind her. "Our foreman will take you to get your belongings and escort you off the property."

"Where am I supposed to go?" Mike sputtered. "I didn't do anything wrong."

"I'll book you a room at the Rio Cottages for three days. After that, you're on your own."

Abigail's phone chimed. Kingston could see the anger building in her eyes as she read the text. When she finally looked up, they were burning. "You told me he had you reimburse him thirty thousand dollars. The actual bill of sale was twenty-five hundred. Seems to be a discrepancy."

Jacob walked into the barn and stood behind Letti. He held himself as a man one clearly did not mess with.

"It's a misunderstanding. I—"

"I don't want to hear it," Letti snapped. "Kingston, Abigail, ride the horses over to your brother's clinic. Jacob and I have this. Naomi and the sheriff are on their way."

Kingston handed Sadie's reins over to Abigail.

She nodded as she led Sadie out of the barn, then paused. "Thank you, Kingston. Your quick action saved the day on so many levels." She swung herself up into the saddle. "Don't tell my granddad I said this, but you would make one fine cowboy."

He wanted to blurt out that he would love to be her cowboy, but that nonsense had to be tied down and forgotten.

Just because she was nice to him didn't mean a thing. Abigail was nice to all the underdogs.

Abigail took several deep breaths and looked ahead. She couldn't allow herself to say something she would regret. She'd already said more than she should have. It had been a stressful day, that was all.

A stressful day that Kingston had shared with her. She couldn't close her eyes without seeing her son in the path of an out-of-control horse. Once everything settled, her heart would stop the flip-flops it was making at the memory of Kingston racing to the rescue, then his gentleness with the gelding.

"Are you okay?" The man taking up all her thoughts rode up next to her.

No. "Yes. But that booking was so important to Letti and Naomi. I blew it."

"I'm impressed with how quickly you took care of the problem. Mike rubbed me the wrong way from the start, but I was afraid I was just being territorial, so I didn't do anything about it."

That surprised her. "Really?"

He chuckled as he rubbed Dakota's neck. "I learned at an early age to hide my true feelings."

She wanted to ask why. Was it Juan Carlos or Letti who hadn't given him a safe place to be himself as a child? "Don't hide them on my account. I'm used to all sorts of opinions being thrown at me."

He raised an eyebrow. "And you still manage to live on the same ranch. Most of you in the same house."

"Oh, we disagree and get in each other's way. But at the end of the day, they're ready to pick me up. They're always there, no matter what."

"Counting on family like that must be nice." He sounded sincere.

"I take it for granted sometimes, but I truly appreciate it. I'm pretty sure you have that with Letti and Naomi if you want it."

He nodded. "Maybe." His lips thinned and he looked out over the pasture. "It's still too fresh for me." He blew out a puff of air. "I had a plan, one I had worked on for years to make happen and it's hard to switch. I'm not sure I want to."

"It's tough to rewire what you think your life should be."

The creaking of the saddles and the soft beat of the hooves on the dirt path set a nice rhythm for her. Riding over the ranch usually calmed her, but she still couldn't believe what a disaster today had been.

Was there anything she could do to save the wedding booking? No matter what anyone said, ultimately it had been her responsibility, and yet Kingston had noticed Dakota getting twitchy before she had.

She closed her eyes to stop the spiral of doom. The image of Leo with a thousand-pound animal heading straight toward him took over. Her son had stood on the outside of the group protecting others. She squeezed her lids tighter. She didn't have time to fall apart.

Not now. There was still a job to complete.

The other horse bumped her knee, and a warm hand covered hers.

"Hey. You're shaking. Everyone's okay."

She tried to take a deep breath, but a sob escaped. She

lowered her head and gritted her teeth, trying to get herself under control.

Kingston moved away from her, and she wanted to cry for him to stay. Opening her eyes, she found him standing at her horse's shoulder.

"Come here." He lifted his hands to help her down.

Without hesitation, she swung her leg over and slid to the ground. She was too embarrassed to make eye contact. "This is ridiculous. I don't know what's wrong with me." She was such a liar.

Why? Why was she pretending not to know? Hadn't she just told him to be open and honest with people? But they were talking about family. She had learned the hard way not everyone loved her like her grandfather and brothers.

Once she was on her feet, he wrapped her in a full hug. A safe cocoon of warmth hidden away from the world. It was an all-consuming hug, and she wanted to stay here forever.

"Why do I feel you're over there blaming yourself for all of this? Everyone, including Dakota, is fine. No one was hurt."

"It's my job to make sure everything goes off without a hitch."

"But that's not what has you upset."

How did he know her so well? Without a doubt, Kingston saw her deeper than Daniel ever did. She closed her eyes. He noticed small things her brothers didn't.

"You're right. I was trying to figure out a way to save the booking. I closed my eyes to clear my mind but all I saw was my son in the path of hooves. If you hadn't been there, I..."

The tears started falling. His large hand cradled her head and held her close as she cried. He whispered soothing words, but for the life of her she didn't recognize any.

When the tears finally dried up, she took a cleansing breath. Stepping out of his arms should happen now, but she wasn't ready to move away from his warmth.

Once she did, it would be over. They should not be this close. But she wanted to linger in the security of his arms. It was exhausting to always stand alone and be strong.

She took a deep breath. Since the end of her marriage, she had made sure Leo never saw her cry. Her brothers were so worried about her they watched her for any cracks. She didn't dare let any show.

"I think you might be having an adrenaline crash." His voice was in her ear, low and gentle. "And you probably know that more than likely Dakota would have avoided them and swerved. Did you notice Leo didn't panic? He was helping."

She nodded. "I think that terrified me more than anything else. The men in my life have taught him well."

"His mom did well too. Some might say we made a good team."

Team. She had thought she had been on a team with Daniel, but she'd ended up alone. Everything in her shouted to trust Kingston and draft him right now, but if he was going to move away, why bother?

"Abigail. You've helped me so much since I arrived. It's been a wild ride and you've encouraged me to hang on and see it through."

"God is the one who will see us through. Even the best families aren't perfect. But when I remember to put my faith in the Lord…" She let her faith settle deep into her bones. Opening her eyes, she lifted her gaze to Kingston. He was staring at her with such intensity it took her breath.

She blinked as he moved closer. His hand cupped her cheek. He looked at her with such longing it turned her insides to mush. To keep her balance, she placed a hand on his arm.

"Can I kiss you?" His voice was so low it took her a minute to process the words.

Not wanting to waste time with a single word, she pressed her lips to his. How was it possible he made her feel treasured with one single kiss? Suddenly, she stepped back. What was she doing? "I'm sorry."

She turned to her saddle, but her legs were too weak to mount.

"No. I..." He picked up Dakota's reins. "I'm sorry. You were upset. I shouldn't have done that."

Keeping her back to him, she rested her forehead on the saddle. "I think I need to walk. It's not far. Can we walk the rest of the way?"

"Sure. Are you okay? I—"

"It's been a long day and I still need to get Leo." Reins in hand, she headed up the path and through the gate. It was about a ten-minute walk.

She could do this. Strong-and-steady Abigail was back.

Chapter Thirteen

Kingston kept his distance following Abigail up the hill to a large metal barn with several paddocks running along the side. At the opposite end it looked as if there was a covered arena.

Isaac, her twin brother, was not alone. *Great.*

Joaquin stood behind the smaller brother, arms crossed, letting it be known he was there to protect his family. He wasn't much taller than Kingston, but man, he was a brick wall of muscle. And the two large dogs standing on guard next to him looked ready to attack. Lucas leaned against a pole, braiding strips of leather. At least he was pretending to have a reason to be there.

Isaac's gaze scanned the horses then quickly went to Abigail before he focused on the horse again. He frowned. "Are you hurt?"

"No. Why?" She self-consciously smoothed her hair and adjusted her glasses.

"You've been crying." Lucas straightened, dropping the nonchalant act. Her two older brothers turned hard glares to Kingston.

He pressed his lips together, resisting the dangerous urge to yell that yes, she had been crying, and they had kissed.

That wouldn't go over well.

She gave an exasperated sigh. "It's been a hard day. People almost got hurt. We lost a huge client. It would have been worse if not for Kingston."

She turned to Dakota and rubbed his muzzle. "I had Mike Davis fired today based on the information you gave me. This is Dakota, the horse I was telling you about. We were told he was from the Childress Ranch. A balloon popped on the other side of a large pasture, and he went ballistic like he was fighting for his life."

Joaquin made a motion to the dogs, and they dropped to their bellies. Was that a better position to attack?

Joaquin caught him looking at his dogs. "I train service dogs. They won't hurt you." He paused. "Unless I order them to."

With that he joined his brothers and eased closer to the gelding. Lucas was the farthest from the horse. "He seems good now."

She nodded in agreement then pointed to Kingston. "Because he acted fast. After getting the rider safely to her feet, he went after him. Dakota jumped a fence and was running straight for Leo and a group of kids from church camp. Kingston cut him off and took him to the round pen. It was incredible to watch."

Joaquin raised an eyebrow as he fed the gelding an alfalfa cube.

Isaac didn't seem to be listening. He ran his hands over every inch of the gelding, talking in low tones the whole time. Was he asking the horse questions?

Isaac moved to the horse's back legs and picked up a hoof. "He has several old injuries. He wasn't fully developed when they happened. How did he respond to you?"

Isaac never looked up, but Kingston assumed he was asking him since he was the only one to have ridden Dakota. "He's smart and well trained. Once I got him to focus on me, he calmed down and did everything I asked."

"You made him feel safe." The vet stood and took the saddle off. He held it out and Lucas took it from him. "The saddle doesn't fit him right. I'll keep him for now until you decide what y'all want to do with him."

He led the horse into the barn without another word.

The two remaining brothers just stared at Kingston.

He cleared his throat. "Abigail, take the rest of the day off. Thanks for helping with Dakota."

"I have to go back. Leo and my car are there, and I need to check in with Letti."

"I have a trailer hooked up to my truck if you want to load the mare." Then Joaquin left. His dogs followed. Did the pair of Akitas give him a departing glare?

"Is he getting his truck?"

"Looks like it," Abigail answered, but she wouldn't meet his gaze. Not letting that wound his pride, he busied himself loosening Sadie's cinch.

"Heads up." Lucas came back from dropping off the saddle and tossed a cube to him.

"Thanks." He offered it to the mare.

"You still have that dog and cat, or did you dump them off somewhere?" Lucas asked.

"I've given up the delusion that I'm finding them a new home. They're mine. Or more like, I belong to them."

With a grunt, Lucas glanced at his sister. "You're okay? I can go with them and pick up Leo and your car. Go to the house and destress."

Kingston bristled at the idea that his home was what caused her stress, or maybe it was him. He frowned. When had he started thinking of the ranch as his home?

"I promised Leo I would have lunch with him. I missed

that, but I can still go hang out during their last activity of the day." She paused. "He was there, Lucas. The horse was running straight at him, but he didn't panic. He was helping the other kids that were scared. You would have been proud of him."

Lucas smiled. "That's my little man. He's a DeLeon." He gave Kingston a level stare. "We take care of others instead of using them."

"You mean when my mother came to your family after Diego's death and the DeLeons turned their backs on her?"

"That's not what happened." Lucas took a step toward him. "She set him up to get the land."

"Really? Why? To sell it? Why did she leave and not use it? That doesn't add up. Someone isn't telling the whole truth."

Lucas's nostrils flared. "Are you saying my grandfather lied?"

"He was grieving. So was she."

Abigail stepped between them. She placed a delicate hand on her brother's chest. "Lucas, I think there's more to the story than we know. Tito was grieving for his wife, both sons and daughter-in-law. Do you think he was able to see the whole picture clearly?"

Lucas blinked and looked down at her.

"Today, Kingston put himself at risk to make sure no one got hurt. Including your nephew. There's lots of things to be angry about, but this is not one of them."

A black king cab truck pulled up at the barn's entrance. Joaquin got out and opened the trailer.

Kingston took a breath. "Lucas, I'm sorry. I shouldn't have responded. I just, well, she's my mom and I know how much she loved him and is still hurting from losing him."

Lucas gave him a small nod. "I'd defend my mother too." He turned and went into the barn.

Kingston led Sadie into the silver livestock trailer. Joaquin was holding it open for him. Kingston stifled a groan. More brotherly advice was surely coming his way.

"I appreciate you helping today, but my sister has been through a lot. So don't use her to get your kicks playing hero, only to walk away when you're done."

Seriously, her brothers gave her no credit. "Oh, she understands I'm no hero. No worries there. There's nothing between us." He closed up the trailer and shut the truck door on a slightly confused DeLeon. It felt good to get in the last word.

Abigail wanted to jab her brothers in the ribs and step on their bare toes. She'd heard what Joaquin had said and it was so embarrassing. She married *one* wrong guy, and now they thought she'd fall in love with anyone who looked at her.

She let out a low growl.

"Did you say something?" Joaquin had one hand draped over the steering wheel like he was innocent and didn't have a care in the world.

Glancing over her shoulder, she saw Kingston's eyes were closed. The dogs sat at the other end of the bench seat staring at him. She leaned over the console and whispered, "I heard what you said to him. I can't believe you and Lucas were waiting for us. Can't you trust me?"

His eyes went to the rearview mirror then back to the road. "We trust you. We trusted you to go off and get your degree and work in a big city. We don't trust men who don't understand commitment. How long does that pretty boy plan to stick around? Don't look at me like that."

Her brothers made her want to scream. "I'm a stronger person now and I have Leo. So, no regrets."

He took his eyes off the road and turned to her. Their noses almost touched. "You showed up red-eyed and..." He glanced down at the lower part of her face. "Don't tell me nothing has happened between you two. I'm ignoring it because I *do* trust you. Him? I would keep walking if he was caught up in a fast current. Let him be washed out to sea. Good riddance."

She flung herself against the headrest and mirrored Kingston's pose. It was a waste of breath to talk to her brothers, and worse, she hated he was right.

Why was she pretending her heart wasn't already lying on the floor at Kingston's feet, raw and exposed? She had to stop putting herself in his path. She would talk to Naomi and tell her they couldn't work together.

"Drop off?" Joaquin asked, speaking in as few syllables as possible again.

"Do you know where the large show stables are?"

With a nod, he drove through the huge entryway and down the paved road. The differences in their ranches were vast. Would she ever be able to turn theirs into a venue?

Even if she did, they wouldn't be able to compete with Tres Amigos. Her dreams were foolish.

For now, she had a good job she loved, at least for the next year. Her son was happy. But then again, the big account she just lost might change her career plans. What if they sued? Dropping her head between her shoulders, she rubbed her head.

"Headache?" Joaquin asked. He opened the middle console and nodded to his painkillers and an unopened bottle of water.

"Thanks." She took them and swallowed the water. "I

love you. You know that, right? I just don't need you playing the big bad wolf."

"But it's the role I know." Driving past the old hacienda, he whistled. "Major upgrades."

She nodded. "It's going to be gorgeous when their vision is complete."

"That's a matter of opinion. Traditions and history are being trampled over." There was a snarl in his voice.

Kingston sat up. She waited for his comeback to the insult, but he just stared out the window. Joaquin pulled up next to the stables and put the truck in Park. "Need any help unloading?"

"I can handle one horse." He opened the door then paused. "Thank you for taking in Dakota. He's a good horse that was put in a bad situation."

"Isaac's the one you need to thank."

With a nod, Kingston shut the door and went to the back of the trailer.

"Why can't you be nice?"

Joaquin shrugged. "Wolves aren't nice to strangers outside their pack."

Rolling her eyes, she opened the door and jumped down. Why did all her brothers have trucks that needed ladders?

Kingston already had the mare out when she came around the trailer. "I'll take care of her. Go ahead and find Leo. I know how much you need to see him. I'm going to check on Fuego as soon as I get this lady taken care of."

He went into the barn and Joaquin drove away. She was left standing alone. It was like the moments in Kingston's arms had never happened.

She watched the man and horse disappear into the stables. The yearning to follow him was strong. Abigail looked at the sky. *Why do I have a longing in my heart that I have to deny? Can You just remove it?*

Her brother had been right about one thing, as much as she wanted to deny it. She had kissed Kingston. *I know it wasn't smart. Please clear my mind and keep me focused.*

Laughter interrupted her quiet moment with God. A smile eased across her face. Leo was easy for her to pick out of the kids in the event barn. That was where she needed to be.

As she got closer, she scanned the area for her son, but he spotted her first and left his line to run to her.

"Momma! That was awesome. The best day of camp in all of camps. Did you see how Mr. Kingston chased the horse down and then rode him in fancy circles in the arena? He asked me to hold on to Sadie. He said I was trained by real cowboys. And that I did a great job helping the counselor too. I think he was tricking us. Mr. Kingston *is* a real cowboy."

Pushing his wild hair out of his face, she smiled. "I think you might be right."

He looked over her shoulder. "Where is he?"

This was the hard part of being a mother. Not being able to control the world around your child, knowing they would get hurt. "He had to take care of the horses. You know he's going back to Dallas soon." She wanted to warn her son not to let his heart get involved.

She was sure it was too late for her.

Chapter Fourteen

Kington glanced at the time, then he slid his phone into his pocket. He had been talking with Axel for over thirty minutes.

The insurance settlement had been much lower than they had anticipated. Mr. Hawthorn had advised Axel to hire a public adjuster.

Whenever he thought life was going well, something happened to pull the rug out from beneath him. What if he had been standing on the wrong rug and God was redirecting him? Could he leave the dream of training and breeding racehorses behind? Guilt was a heavy weight. Axel had been taking care of everything for over two weeks now.

Fuego nudged him. Kingston leaned in and scratched the big horse's jaw. "Why are we trying to force you onto the track if you don't want to go?"

The horse nodded in agreement. He laughed. "Now I'm having conversations with a horse."

He tilted his head and studied the stallion. "I haven't missed the racetrack either." That was a surprise. But then again, he still worked with horses daily.

The racing scene had never been his dream. It was the horses. Fuego tossed his head and spun around. Then, with a swish of his tail, he lunged forward and ran, making it clear their conversation was over.

The stallion stretched his legs and galloped full-out along the fence line. His red coat gleamed in the sun. He stopped and turned, heading in the other direction. Kingston needed to talk to Axel again.

Plans could change.

The sound of kids cheering carried across the pasture. He had promised Leo he'd stop by and say hi.

And no way was he ever going to be one of those adults who got too busy to keep his word to a kid.

He cut through the pasture and passed the stables, and as he turned on the path to the event barn Letti stopped him. "Let's talk." She gave him a tentative smile.

"Not now. I promised Leo I'd stop by and join him in whatever activity they're doing today. You can walk with me if you want."

"Oh, kids don't notice that kind of thing." Her smile grew brighter as she waved her hand around. "You can catch up with him later."

He stopped and turned to face her. "Do you believe that?"

She blinked and stepped away. "I don't think kids really pay attention to what adults say they'll do."

"Did you ever have an adult abandon you? Promise you to take you somewhere or do something with you, then bail because… I don't know, they got a better offer?"

Her eyes went wide, and she crossed her hands over her chest, palms flat. "Juan Carlos never let me out of his sight. I remember wanting to be left alone." Her attempt at a laugh failed. "I took you with me until Juan Carlos said you needed to stay in school. I agreed. You seemed happy."

He tilted his head and looked at her with total confusion. "You really don't remember not being at school events after you promised me you'd be there. Or the times you were supposed to pick me up and I had to sit in the office for hours waiting. The birthdays and holidays we made plans for, then you just…"

She was blinking. Tears forming. "I know I wasn't a… I wasn't the ideal TV mom. But…" She licked her lips. "Oh, Kingston. I didn't think you cared if I was there or not. You were always serious, but you seemed fine. Even happy. You never said anything."

"I didn't have a choice. When I was younger, I cried, and Juan Carlos told me it would upset *my mom*. When you did take me, I didn't want to cause any trouble. I was taught you were fragile, and I didn't want to break you."

She covered her mouth with one hand as tears slipped down her face.

He closed his eyes and lowered his head. "And now you're crying." He pulled her into his arms. What was wrong with him? "I'm sorry. It's old history. I'm an adult now. But Leo is a kid, and even if he doesn't notice that I broke a promise, I'll know."

His gaze went to the event barn. The kids were sitting at tables. It looked like they were making something. She had stopped crying and with a squeeze let him go. She wiped her face.

He lowered his chin to make eye contact. "I promise we'll talk tonight. Dinner?"

"Yes." Her smile was slight, but better than the tears. "I'll make meat loaf and potatoes."

"My favorite." He didn't want to push her out of the good place she had found at the ranch. "Are you okay? I can text Abigail if you need me to stay."

Straightening her spine, she shook her head. "I'm the one who's sorry. Go to Leo." She took a step closer and brushed his hair back. "I'm so proud of you. Not sure how it happened, but you're a good man. I'll see you tonight."

Turning, she took the path to her home. *Wow.* That emotional storm hit him from nowhere. Packing it away for now, he took the opposite path, which led to child-filled chaos. He stepped into the barn. Before his eyes could adjust, Leo yelled his name.

"Mr. Kingston!" The small form tackled him from the right.

"Hey, Leo. Careful there. You're stronger than you know. We both almost ended up on the floor." He dropped down and smiled at the boy.

"That was so cool what you did with Dakota. I was telling Mom that you played a prank on us. Pretended not to be a cowboy when you were one all along." The little boy laughed. "That's a good joke."

Abigail walked up behind Leo. He twisted around to look at his mom. "See, Mom? I told you Mr. Kingston promised me he'd come."

He looked at Abigail. Had she not believed him? "Your mom doesn't know me well enough yet, but when I make a promise, I keep it."

"Just like a real cowboy." Leo nodded with authority. "Come on, you can make a rain stick with me. Then it's time to go. You should come with us for dinner. You can tell everyone what you did."

This kid did not have the hate-all-Zayases gene like the rest of his family. But before he could say anything, Abigail took Leo's hand.

"What did I say about inviting people without asking the adults? Plus, I'm sure Mr. Kingston has plans already. He doesn't have time to make a rain stick."

Kingston stood. "I'm having dinner with my mom. We

can't let down our moms. But I will take you up on the offer to make a rain stick."

Leo ran ahead to the table he had come from. Abigail still had her back to Kingston. "You don't have to do this. He's not your responsibility. It was nice of you to stop by, but I think it would be better if you kept your distance."

From the table, Leo waved at him. "Your son's waiting for me. I told him I would make a rain stick with him and I will." She turned and they held eye contact, her gaze penetrating.

"I don't make promises I don't keep." With a nod, he walked around her and joined Leo at the table.

As Leo handed him all the supplies, Kingston's eyes stayed on Abigail. She didn't seem to understand what came so naturally to her, being a good mom, was a priceless gift to her son.

Perhaps it was due to the conversation he'd had with his mother, but there was a protective urge he had never experienced before. Kingston wasn't gonna let this little boy down either.

He focused his attention back on Leo as the boy explained how to make a rain stick out of an empty paper towel roll and yarn.

With too much glue, Kingston's blue yarn became a mess. "That's okay. Here." Leo gave him an old rag. "Just wipe it clean and pull your yarn tight. It doesn't have to be perfect if you like it." Leo showed him how to add beads. It was surprisingly fun.

All the kids were excited to see Kingston. He had never been so popular. They all wanted to show him their own rain sticks. Several asked him where he learned to ride horses. Some told him stories about their horses.

He listened to each story and found something unique

about their rain sticks. If anyone had told him a year ago that he'd be sitting in the middle of church camp with a bunch of kids and not wanting to leave, he would've said they had the wrong guy.

He grinned. How did this become his life?

But what if it could be? Across the table, Abigail laughed as her yellow-and-purple yarn fell. A little girl about Leo's age helped her glue it.

He liked the idea that he could be the kind of man who a family could count on. But could he never let them down? That might be the scariest part of it all, but it's what Abigail and Leo deserved.

He studied his rain stick. It was a mess, just like him. Pushing the yarn into place, he tried to even out the lines and smooth them down.

It reminded him of his unfortunate wirehaired mutt. She wasn't perfect, but she had worked his way into his heart. And the kitten, who pretended to be hostile until she was purring in his arms. They depended on him now.

For the first time, he had real family connections. It was strange knowing his cousin was his birth mom, but it helped to understand his mother better.

Abigail was right. Letti would always be the mother of his heart. No matter how much she had messed up, he had never stopped loving her or wanting her love.

Ironically, for the first time, he could truly feel that love. Was there a future here for him? Maybe he could stay for the year to make sure the inheritance stipulation was met, then he could focus on rebuilding with Axel. One year wasn't that long. It would give Axel and him the time to make sure they did it right.

Was he just looking for excuses to stay? He took a deep breath. One year.

Where would that leave Abigail and Leo?

No, this ranch life was temporary. He didn't have the skill set to be the man they needed full-time. For life. What would happen to them when he messed up and let them down?

Abigail forgot what she was doing as she watched Kingston. He was making it hard not to like him. Or was she just doing the opposite of what her brothers wanted?

Each camper who came up to Kingston got his full attention. The kids adored him. She didn't think her heart could take any more. The head counselor called for everyone's attention and gathered the kids in a big circle to do a few activities with the rain sticks.

"Wow. The rice does sound like rain," Kingston said as he followed the directions. "I need to use it on the nights I can't sleep." His eyes sparkled with joy as he smiled at her.

And her heart did a stupid flip-flop. "You act as if this is your first time at camp."

He laughed. "This kind of camp, it is. Growing up, I went to sports camps or computer camps. There were a few riding camps that I enjoyed because of the horses. But they were intense and highly competitive. It was all about prep for a select college my uncle thought I needed. I guess my grandfather, now. It's so weird to shift that connection. He knew he was my grandfather but didn't think I needed to know."

"He's gone, so it's up to you to decide who he is to you." She inwardly rolled her eyes at herself. Just like the rest of her family, she thought people needed unasked-for advice. "Not that my opinion matters."

"My new life motto. Words of truth are always welcome."

"You'll get plenty of that if you stick around." She turned her face away. "Sorry. I know you're not staying."

He opened his mouth to say something, but Leo ran between them. "We're all done! Can I go see Mr. Kingston's dog and cat? Tio Lucas says it's a rat dog."

"Leo. You can't invite yourself to someone's house."

"I didn't. I asked." His forehead wrinkled. "How do people know what I want if I don't ask?"

"He's got a point." Kingston squeezed Leo's shoulder. "And the answer is yes. You can visit Little Momma and Baby. But you're not allowed to call her a rat dog. She's a survivor who deserves respect."

Abigail groaned. Her plan to keep her distance from him was going as well as the other ones.

"Yay! Let's go." Leo took her hand and pulled her along the path to the bunkhouse. Kingston didn't even have a real home. It was temporary housing.

She moved too slowly for her son. He dropped her hand and ran ahead.

Kingston laughed as he came up beside her. "I don't think I've ever had that kind of energy."

"Aren't you the one who said you didn't like kids when we first met?" That sounded a little more snappish than it had seemed in her head.

"I said I wasn't good with kids, but it would have been more accurate to say I had no experience with kids."

"Then you're a natural. Or maybe you're still a kid yourself and can relate to them on their level."

"I'm not sure I was ever a kid. I'm truly surprised how much I enjoyed today."

Leo made it onto the porch, then climbed up the railing. He walked on it like a balance beam, but being raw cedar post, it wasn't flat.

Kingston whistled. "That kid of yours has some impressive agility."

"Don't tell him that. It'll only encourage him." She cupped her hands around her mouth. "Leo! Get down from there. You could break something."

Swinging on the post, he jumped down. Kingston went to unlock the door, and both of their phones chimed.

"That was weird," he said as he opened the door and stepped aside for them to enter.

"It's Naomi. She texted us both." Her stomach dropped. Was it bad news?

The sound of running paws on the floor welcomed them. Leo went to his knees. After the dog greeted Kingston, sniffing him to make sure all was good, she turned to Leo.

Her son was all grins. "Come here, girl."

The little dog didn't hesitate to jump on him. Her stubbed tail wagged her whole body as she licked his face. "She likes me." He giggled.

"That she does. She doesn't just kiss anyone. The little lady is very picky."

"As she should be." Abigail couldn't help but smile at her son's joy.

Kingston picked up the kitten and tucked her into his arm. A loud purring filled the space as he scratched her ears and chin. "What's the text? I'm supposed to meet them for dinner in a couple of hours."

"Oh, the text." Stalling never made anything better. Abigail opened the text and read it, then read it again. Was she reading it right?

"Abigail?" He set the kitten down and came over to her and placed a hand under her elbow.

Her brain had to be playing tricks on her. This time she read it out loud. "'Zeta was so impressed with the vision you shared with her and with Kingston's heroics that she asked if he would lead their mini cattle drive.'" She lifted her gaze to meet his. "They booked the ranch for a five-day event next fall."

She jumped up and down, then threw her arms around him. "We did it! We got the account!"

He spun her around. When he stopped, so did time. Staring into each other's eyes, they just stood there. She forgot to breathe.

Leo and Little Momma joined in on the excitement and collided with her. She bent down and hugged her son, breaking all contact with Kingston. "I'm so happy, Momma. I want to go on a cattle drive. What's a booking?"

"It means your mom is good at her job." He stepped back and leaned on the edge of the table, his ankles crossed.

"It means that Mr. Kingston's—" she smiled at him and lingered in his gaze "—wild ride across the pasture and over the fence saved more than just the day. He saved my job."

"Not true." He bent down, picked up the kitten then went to a cabinet. "Your mom's the best." He pulled a canister of treats out and handed a couple to Leo. "Here. She likes these." Then he got some nuggets for the kitten. "She managed to take a catastrophe and turn it into a win for everyone. Even Dakota."

"Our wrangler would not agree. He lost his job today."

"As he should have."

Leo held up the last treat and the small dog sat up. "Look what I taught her to do! Mr. Kingston, you should be the new wrangler." He tilted his head and looked up at his new hero. "What do you do at the ranch?"

Kingston chuckled. "I ride to the rescue and make rain sticks."

"No. I mean for real." Leo stood, holding the dog.

"I'm upgrading the venue's website."

"Website? That doesn't sound fun. You should tell Miss Letti you want to be the wrangler. You're good with horses. And you can do cattle drives like that lady wants."

"Leo, he probably won't be here by then."

"I don't know. I—"

"Mr. Kingston has racehorses in Dallas." She cut off any potential false hope he was going to give her son. "That's where he lives."

Leo frowned. "I thought you had to live here for a year. That's what Gloria and Jacob said."

"Leo, what did I say about listening to other people's conversations and then repeating them?"

"It's gossip and we don't do that. But what about the ranch? If they lose it, will you have a job? And what about Little Momma and Baby? This is their home. I don't want them to leave." He hung his head to hide his tears. "I don't want Mr. Kingston to leave."

And her heart officially broke. Sinking to her knees in front of her son, she put her hands on his shoulders. She glanced over at Kingston. His face was stone. She had known this would happen. Another man would walk out of her son's life. Her life.

"Mr. Kingston has to do what is right for him. People will always come and go in our lives."

The tall man standing above them dropped to the ground. He crossed his legs and let the kitten curl up there. "Leo. What if I did stay? I—"

"Don't." She shot him her hardest glare. It might have broken the record of anything she had given her brothers. "Don't say something to make right now easier on you."

He nodded. "I get that. I spent my whole childhood waiting for an adult to see me. I learned that words are empty."

"You want to stay?" Leo asked after a loud sniff.

"I do. I don't want to leave my mom and Naomi in a bad spot. They need me and I think I need them right now. But I have my best friend, Axel, in Dallas. He needs me too. So, I'm trying to figure out how I can be there for all of them. I don't want you to cry." He took a deep breath and laid a fist over his heart. "That hurts me right here."

"I'm sorry. I didn't mean to hurt you. I just got sad at you going away. My dad left too. He didn't say goodbye. One morning I woke up, went down to get breakfast and he was gone. Momma acted like she was happy about it. She said we would be moving to the ranch."

"Oh, baby, no. I..." She covered her mouth, words failing her. That had been the worst night of her life. While she was tucking Leo into bed, Daniel had packed. He said it would be easier for Leo this way. She had yelled that it was easier for Daniel.

After he'd walked out of their home, she'd fallen on the sofa and cried all night. When the sun peeked through the windows, she'd taken a shower and gone to the kitchen to fix Leo his favorite breakfast. Ready to do anything to make Leo feel safe.

"I imagine she didn't want to upset you. She was probably very sad but covered it up."

She nodded. "I was."

"We moved to the ranch before Dad came back. Does he know I'm here?"

Lips pressed shut, she held in the heart-wrenching gasp. Her son thought she had taken him from his father and hidden him.

"He knows." Kingston spoke with authority even though

he didn't know. But he knew her, she realized. She would never hide her son from his father.

"Your dad is like a bunch of the people who loved and raised me," Kingston said in a low voice.

Leo crawled into Kingston's lap. Adjusting the kitten and her son, he settled them in and put an arm around Leo. Her little man looked so tiny curled into Kingston's tall frame. Not wanting to be left out, Little Momma joined them and gave Leo a few kisses.

"What do you mean?"

"Well, they loved me, but didn't know how to be there for me. Even though they were adults, there were big issues in their lives that got in the way of being the adult. When I was a kid, I thought it was because I…" There was a waver in his voice she had not heard before.

"You had done something bad, so they didn't love you."

"Yes." He visibly swallowed. "But now I know it had nothing to do with their love for me. It was things I had no control over. I don't know what your dad is dealing with in his life, but I promise it has nothing to do with what you have done. You are very lovable. You're smart, funny and good at so many things."

"Mom says I have too much energy."

Abigail said, "Oh, baby. I love you just the way you are. There is nothing you could ever do to make me stop loving you."

He nodded. "God loves me too. And Tito, Emma and all my uncles. Moving to the ranch is the best thing ever. I don't want to ever leave. I just wish Daddy would visit." He twisted to look up at Kingston. "You should stay here forever."

"It is one of the best places on Earth. I don't know where I'm supposed to be right now. But I can promise you that

I won't leave without saying goodbye. Even if I go to Dallas, I'll be back."

"How far is Dallas?"

"If you ate breakfast, then got in the car, you would be there before dinner."

"That's not too far."

Abigail shifted to face Kingston. Her son's eyes fluttered closed. "He's sleepy. Let me get him."

"He's fine."

Abigail leaned in. Kingston's whisper was so low she could barely hear him.

"I, um, think I kind of need this too." He looked at Leo with such sadness and longing that her heart broke for all of them.

"Thank you for everything you said. I…" She licked her dry lips. "I had no clue that was how he had interpreted Daniel's leaving. I thought I was protecting him. Leo, not Daniel."

"I know." They fell into silence.

A soft knock was followed by Letti poking her head in. "Hello? King—oh. Hi, Abigail." She turned to talk to someone behind her. "Abigail's here." Facing them again, she smiled. "We'll come back later."

Abigail stood. "No. No, come in. Leo had a long day. He fell asleep in Kingston's lap."

Naomi came in behind Letti. They were both carrying shallow boxes. "Oh. My heart just melted. Is that not the dearest sight?"

The women put the boxes on the counter. "We thought it would be fun to have dinner at your place for once," Letti said as she glanced around the bunkhouse. "We need to get you in a real home or update this one."

He stood, holding Leo to him so he didn't wake up. "I

was living in a make-do apartment above the stables. This is fine."

"Do you want me to take him? We can leave."

"Oh no. This is a celebration dinner," Naomi said. "With you two working as a team, we booked the biggest event yet and now we have to get ready to deliver everything we promised them."

"Stay. I'll lay him down on the sofa." Kingston gently rose while holding her son.

"What about you?" Letti grinned at her own son. "Does this mean you're staying on? You can be our wrangler and lead the cattle drive next fall."

"I need to talk to Axel, but I think we can manage something for the next year."

Eyes wide, both women looked shocked and thrilled, but he held his hand up. "Before you get too excited, I'm not staying long-term. I made a commitment first to Axel."

The two women exchanged glances and then nodded at him. "That's all we asked for." They looked at Abigail. "No uncertainty left for the venue. We can plan full steam ahead."

They started setting the table and chatting about the upcoming events.

Abigail sat next to her sleeping son. She would set limits. Kingston never lied. He was clear about not staying permanently. If he was honest with them, she could do this.

She had survived Daniel walking out on them. Kingston wasn't doing that. If she focused on her son and life goals, it would be okay.

She would be okay.

Chapter Fifteen

Kingston stepped into the event barn and shook the rain off his slicker. Rain pounded on the roof and pooled on low areas outside. It had been raining off and on for the last three days. The weather report had said it would clear up today. But the system creating the storm had stalled and they were being slammed again.

Abigail had moved the latest wedding into the barn and thrown up every fairy light she could find. Lanterns gleamed on the tables and hung from ceiling beams. Bundles of white flowers had turned everything into a secret fantasy land. The bride and groom had even taken the black-and-pink umbrellas Abigail had offered and taken some epic pictures in the rain.

The party of eighty had danced for the last hour and a half. Now they were going to have to get all the guests off the ranch before they were trapped.

Jacob lowered his hood as he nodded at Kingston. "I got another row of sandbags stacked. Cindy just pulled up with a school bus."

"How did she manage that?" The woman was a walking Swiss Army knife.

"She has connections." Jacob grinned.

At the front of the large space, Abigail moved to the DJ

platform and took the mic. "Y'all have been the best. This is a wedding none of us will forget." Everyone cheered. "I can't wait to see the pictures. The rain is heavier than predicted. We have everything taken care of, but the crossing at the front of the ranch is rising."

She looked over at Kingston and he gave her a thumbs-up. With a smile, she nodded. "We have brought in transportation to get everyone safely to Rio Bella. The Bella Lodge is waiting for you with dinner. If you make your way to the door, Jacob will escort you to the bus."

Kingston stayed with Jacob and chatted with everyone waiting for their turn to board the bus. Several thanked him for making the day special despite the weather. He gave all the credit to Abigail. With the last group gone, he headed across the room.

She handed the mic to the local DJ, who had to be about sixteen. Emma DeLeon was with her, helping pack up.

When he arrived at the foot of the stage, Abigail grabbed his arm. Her easygoing appearance was a thin top cover. "I moved the newlyweds to Treetop Cabin. I'm taking them up there now. It's smaller but completely out of any flooding zones. I stocked it earlier. They might have to stay locked away for a few days, but they seem fine with that."

"Cindy left for town. What do you need me to do?"

"Help Harley and Emma with anything they have to load and make sure they get out safely." She jumped down. "Tell Emma to call me when she gets home."

She closed her eyes and took a deep breath.

"It's going to be okay, Abigail. We've got this. I'm used to extreme weather in Dallas. I've even been known to run into a burning barn to save horses. We're good."

Her face relaxed and he almost got a smile out of her.

She pointed at him. "No burning barns today. If you

could get Leo for me, he's at the office with Gloria. Can you take him to the large stables? It's our sturdiest building. The office will probably be fine, but if it gets worse the stable has a loft and is designed to keep flood waters out. It also has a landline and a generator if we lose electricity."

"Got it. I'll meet you there." He wanted to hug her and reassure her she had handled the unexpected like a pro. But she had drawn a clear line between them.

The girls were at the back of the stage. He scanned the equipment. At least it wasn't much. "What can I help load? Are you going to be okay getting out of here?"

Harley grinned at him. "Thanks, but I just have these." She pointed to the two cases she and Emma held. "Abigail said I could leave the speakers and get them later. I have Grandma Cindy's orange beast, so the crossing won't be a problem."

"You're related to Cindy? She's one tough cookie." He turned to Emma. "Abigail wants you to call as soon as you get home." He smirked. "And tell your grandfather she's safe with me."

Emma laughed—she looked just like her aunt. "Are you sure you want me to tell him that?"

The rain paused and they looked up to the ceiling like they could see the storm. "Maybe it finally stopped." A loud boom rattled the whole place. The overhead lights flickered, then went out. They would have been plunged into darkness except for the hundreds of fairy lights that were acting as candles.

"That's not good. Wonder if it's out all over the area or just this building?" He followed the girls to make sure they got into the Suburban without any trouble. While he watched them drive away, he tried calling Letti. She didn't answer so he tried Naomi. No answer. It looked as if the lights were out in the other buildings.

It started raining again. He threw the hood of his yellow slicker over his hat and went to the pole barn where they kept the vehicles. Grabbing one of the off-road vehicles would be the fastest way around.

Naomi ran from the covering, head ducked to avoid the rain. She saw him and stopped. "Are the guests evacuated? Where's Abigail?"

Kingston took her hand and went under the metal roof. The rain was hitting it so hard, and they had to yell.

"They're loaded on a bus heading to town. Cindy'll call once they get everyone to the lodge. Abigail is taking the newlyweds to Treetop Cabin using the four-by-four." He held his hand up to block the rain the wind pushed into the shelter. "I'm getting Leo and Gloria to take them to the stables."

"That's good. It's the safest place."

"Do you need help with the sandbags?"

"No. We used all the ones we had. Hopefully, they'll help. I'm running to the barns," she shouted over the rain. "We have another problem though."

"Yeah, I know. The electricity is out."

"It is? Great. No, I was talking about the two hundred pasture. When we were at the Pecan Grove cabins, the river was much higher than we anticipated. Fifty cattle need to be moved now. Letti's already down there with Sadie. I'm trading my truck for a horse. It's too muddy down there for anything with wheels. They'll be trapped between the river and the fence in another couple of hours or less if we don't get them."

"Can't you just open the gate?"

"A few are by the fence line already, but a lot of them are

hiding. We have to flush them out." She wiped rain from her eyes.

He grabbed the keys to the yellow UTV they called Bumble Bee. "I'll give you a ride."

"Thanks."

It didn't take them long to get out of the shed, but getting around the water was another story. "Thanks for helping. All the workers left to take care of their places."

He nodded.

"Kingston?" she said over the rain.

"Yeah?"

"I want you to know that I understand if you don't know how to feel about me." She held on to the sidebar and braced herself as he jumped some rocks to avoid running water. "You know I'm your birth mother now, but that doesn't change that Letti's still your mother. We all messed up and your childhood paid the highest price. I'm so sorry for the role I played in that."

His hands gripped the wheel. What was he supposed to do with this right now? His brain, just like this rain runoff, was all over the place, making new paths and out of control.

It was an overload of thoughts and emotions.

"I know you didn't want to come to the ranch," she continued. "Thank you for sticking it out and not running, like we did to you."

"You were just a kid too." His anger wasn't directed at her or his mom. "Juan Carlos is a coward for waiting till after he died to come clean."

A sound that could have been a laugh came from her. "I agree. All I want to say is I'm so proud of you and love you. You can do with that what you want. I'm here for you in any way you need. No strings or expectations."

Rain hit him in the face as he dodged the biggest areas of

water. Rapids were flowing like wild rivers in newly made trenches. At this rate, they were all going to be swimming. He pulled up next to the double doors, and she hopped out.

"Thank you for giving us a chance to make it up to you."

"You're family. We're here for each other." He thought she might start to cry, but with a quick nod, she ran inside the barn.

He hit the gas and got to the office as fast as he could.

Leo was on the sofa reading a picture book with a flashlight. He had never seen the kid sit so still. Gloria was standing next to the fireplace and looking out the window.

"Abigail said to move y'all to the stables. Do you have a rain slicker?"

She opened the closet door.

"Yay!" Leo jumped up. "I wanted to go out in the rain, but Ms. Gloria said no." He ran to her and let her put a smallish raincoat on him. It still swallowed him, but the kid smiled. "How do I look?"

Kingston gave him a nod. "Like a real cowboy, ready to ride to the rescue." Without thought, he picked up the kid and headed to the door.

"Hurry, Ms. Gloria, get your rain gear on."

Leo in his arms, he ran from the steps into the UTV. Gloria slid into the back seat, trying to avoid the deluge of rainfall. Kingston handed Leo to her.

He had always scoffed at the cars with the stickers that said Precious Cargo. Now he got it.

Leo leaned forward and tugged on his arm then pointed to his bunkhouse. "Should we get Little Momma and Baby? They're probably scared."

There was a large covering over the back door, so he stopped under it.

"I'll get them." Leo had his seat belt undone and was jumping off his seat.

Gloria sounded as if she was praying. His phone chimed. Checking, he saw a text from Cindy.

All the guests were safe and sound at the lodge, enjoying the best Mexican food this side of the border. He smiled and put his phone away. Leo came out with the two wrapped in Baby's favorite blanket. He took the bundle so Leo could get his seat belt on.

The kitten was buried deep in the fabric, but Little Momma had her head out, her lopsided ears trembling. "Sorry I left you alone in the storm." He rubbed his forehead against hers.

Leo reached for them and settled the duo in his lap. "We rescued them! On to the stables."

When they arrived, Abigail was running from the old four-by-four to the barn doors. She opened them wide enough for him to drive straight in. The barn was dark but dry.

Shelter from the storm. She rushed to her son and hugged him and kissed his forehead.

Abigail made sure Leo was secure in his mother's love, even with his father leaving like he did. She was steadfast and sturdy.

She deserved that in a partner. Was he capable of being that solid for her? Life was always going to bring storms to their door. He wanted to be their shelter.

Abigail wanted to hug Kingston too. He looked so lost. "Are you okay? Is something wrong? Someone hurt?"

"Cindy got everyone to town safely. I'm fine." He said the words, but she didn't believe him.

"I heard from Emma. They made it to the house." She

knelt in front of her son and pushed the wet hair from his precious face. "I missed you. Are you good?"

He grinned and nodded rapidly. "Kingston made me wear a rain slicker like his. See?" He held his bundle closer. "I rescued Little Momma and Baby. I want to help move the cows. He said I'm a cowboy ready to ride."

"Oh no. You're staying here." She glanced up at Kingston and bit back a smile. The guilty expression on his face reminded her of her brothers when they were afraid she was going to be mad.

He shut off the engine. "I'm going to get the generator going." He hopped out of Bumble Bee.

"I'll get the generator." Gloria climbed out and headed to the storage room. "Y'all get horses saddled. The ladies need you. I'll keep an eye on *mijo*."

"They have to move the herd out of the lower pasture," he told her. Abigail's eyes went wide for a moment, then she moved into action. He followed. She had saddled Ruby, and he had Goldy ready by the time Gloria was back. The lights were on.

As they passed the last stall, Fuego greeted her by putting his head over the door. "Good boy." She rubbed his muzzle. "He's adjusted well."

"He has. But as much as I know he wants to run, I don't think he's ready to help round up cattle in this mess."

She laughed. "That would be a sight. Maybe he's more cow horse than racehorse."

They rode out side by side, pushing the horses as fast as they safely could. They saw Letti first. She had a herd of about forty cows and calves.

"Naomi went down. We're still missing some." Her voice was almost drowned out by the roar of the usually serene river.

Kingston stood in his saddle and scanned the area below them. The normally clear Frio was dark and murky. It had escaped its banks and the tall tree whose roots he had sat on were underwater. The top of the tree swayed as the river rushed around it. Giant tree trunks had been uprooted and were now tossed by the raging river as if they were nothing more than toothpicks. The river was swallowing everything in its path, and that path was getting wider. It was a terrifying sight.

"There she is." Abigail pointed to Naomi as she guided a couple of cows to them.

"Come on," Abigail called out to him as she rode to the edge of a cedar break.

He pulled up next to her, scanning the area. "How do we get them out?"

"They're scared and won't easily be moved. Goldy is a smart cow horse. Get behind them and let her do her thing. You ride well, so just move with her."

He nodded and waited. Abigail went in and drove a cow and her calf out of a clump of juniper. His horse moved in and pushed them to the northwest. The momma tried to turn back, but his horse was ready and cut her off. Naomi moved in to push the pair to the fence.

The cow saw the other cattle gathered and ran to them, her baby by her side.

"I don't know if we are going to be able to find them all." The rain didn't hide the fact Naomi was crying. "We're still missing four. I can't stand the thought of leaving one of them behind to be taken by the river."

He nodded. "We'll go along the fence line as far as we can go. You join Letti and get the ones we've gathered onto higher ground."

Naomi nodded and turned, then stopped. She pointed. "What are they doing here?"

Kingston and Abigail turned at the same time.

Cyrus, Joaquin, Lucas, Isaac and Tito rode over the top of the hill on horseback. They made an impressive sight against the moody sky. It was like one of their Western movies. Cowboys to the rescue. The urge to cry in relief overwhelmed her. They had come to help her and the Zayas family without her asking.

Kingston's horse tossed her head and pranced in place when he pulled her next to Abigail. "Oh no. What did she tell him?"

Frowning, she looked at him. Rain dripped from the edge of his cowboy hat. "What do you mean?"

"When I told Emma to call you, I also said to give your grandfather a message. That you were safe with me. I was kind of joking, but it might have put them on the warpath."

Pride filled her. "They do make an intimidating sight."

"Isaac's riding Dakota," Kingston said.

Cyrus and Lucas rode forward. They nodded to Naomi. "Emma said y'all were short-staffed and needed to move cattle from the river pasture." Cyrus pointed to the north. "The easiest way to get them out of this pasture is through the gate over there. It's the widest and it's a more direct path up to high ground. Do you have them all?"

"That's your property," Naomi stated.

"Yes, ma'am. And this used to be ours too. We built all these fences. That's going to be the fastest way to get them out of here. Do you want our help or not?" He crossed his hand over his saddle horn and stared down Naomi as if he had all day and the rain wasn't dripping off him.

Abigail wanted to roll her eyes.

"Thank you. We're still missing a few," Letti yelled as she joined them.

With a nod, Cyrus lifted his arm and made a motion to his brothers and grandfather. "They'll move these cattle while we find your stragglers."

With her family's help, they got the whole herd to safer grounds. Isaac followed them to the stables as the rest of her family returned home.

They paused to look down at the river. The fence post had vanished. Her stomach bottomed out at the display of power.

"Thank God, we got them out in time," Naomi said, then clicked her horse into a gallop.

Abigail was happy to see the stables. She needed time to decompress and just hold her son. Today, Kingston had been there for her at every turn. Her heart wanted to ask him to stay, but her mind knew it was pointless.

Gloria was running toward them. "You're back! I went to the restroom and when I came out Leo and the little dog were gone. I've called and called. I can't find them any-where."

Chapter Sixteen

All the blood drained from Kingston's face as he looked over at Abigail. Her face had lost all color too. She swung off her horse, dropped the reins and ran to the stables. As she went, she yelled all the places in the stables he could be. Gloria shook her head. She had already looked there.

Kingston was off his horse and about to run after Abigail, but he stopped and took in the three people around him, all looking as lost as he felt. "Isaac, call Cyrus. Tell him we can't find Leo. Naomi, you and Letti search the area around the stables and check the buildings close by."

Picking up Ruby's reins, he rushed to the barn, leading the two horses at a trot. Abigail stood in the middle of the aisle. Gloria was crying and kept apologizing.

"Isaac's calling Cyrus. I'm sure they'll be here soon. Letti and Naomi are searching around the barn and all the buildings close by. He can't be far."

"He wanted to help. You told him he was ready." She looked at him. "What if he went to the river to look for cattle?"

The fear in her eyes pierced his heart—a heart that stopped beating at the thought.

"I'm going to hit the south path to the river," she said. "If he wanted to help, he might have gone that way."

"I'll hit another trail." He put each horse in a stall. "Which—"

"No, stay here," she snapped. "I don't need you getting lost too."

He watched until she was a blurred silhouette in the gray drizzle. She blamed him, and she was right. Wanting to make Leo happy, he had told him he was ready to do cowboy work.

Leo was out there alone. The possibilities were too devastating to consider. He walked to the other end of the barn. "Gloria, where was the last place you saw Leo?"

"Right where you're standing. I told him not to move." Tears were falling again.

"He can be a little headstrong." He put a hand on her shoulder. "Have you met his family?"

She laughed. It was a bit brittle, but it was better than tears. "Yes." She closed her eyes and prayed.

He studied the landscape. Where could Leo have gone? "I'm going to look a little farther out."

He flipped his hood up and swung his gaze across the ground. All he saw was a mess of hoofprints. He circled farther out and finally came across a small boot print.

The flat grassy area turned into a rocky cedar break that gradually went up into a rocky hill. "Why would Leo go this direction?" It was heading away from any buildings. As he walked on, he found another boot print and paw prints.

He had never learned the different types of tracks. He thought one was Little Momma, but what was the other one? Could be a random raccoon or mountain lion as far as he knew. His heart rate spiked. He took out his phone and tried Abigail, then Letti and Naomi. No one answered.

At one point, he lost track of the prints and had to double back. The boot prints and paw prints were zigzagging around the bottom of the rocky hill. Then he realized they were following a deer trail. He came to a fence.

He called Leo's name and waited. Nothing. Was the boy heading home? If so, it was the hardest way to get there. Hopping the fence, he picked up the trail again.

Then he heard it. He paused to make sure. *Yes.* It was Little Momma's bark. Running to the sound, he called for her.

The barking became frantic, but he didn't see her. Stopping, he slowed his breath. "Leo?"

"We're down here."

Down? Twisting, he looked up at the slope behind him.

"We're in a hole."

"Keep talking. I'm following your voice. Why did you leave the barn?"

"I saw a kitten. It was wet and looked scared. I was going to rescue it, but Little Momma scared it off. I have it now. It's in my raincoat. Is Baby okay? Did she stay in the barn?"

A huge rock, taller than Kingston, had slid down the hillside. A couple of trees were roots up. "She's with Gloria."

"I didn't know there was a hole. I went under the roots of the tree by the big rock, then the ground fell. I'm on a flat rock but when I try to climb up, mud and water fall on me." He started crying. "I can't get out."

"It's okay. I'm here. Can you see the sky?"

"Yes. But the ground keeps falling. The hole is really deep. I can hear water like a river. I don't want to fall into the river. It's dark. Kingston, please get me."

Every fiber of his being wanted to rush in and grab him. "I'm right here, buddy." He looked around for a safe way to get closer. He lowered himself to the ground and felt around for any weaknesses or openings. The mud slid under him, and he backed off. He needed to get to the other side of the trees. Then maybe he could see the situation.

Going around the rock, he saw what the dense branches of the upturned cedar and the rock had been hiding.

There was a gaping cavern and Leo was perched on a ledge. He fell to his stomach and crawled as close as he could without disturbing the loose earth. "Hey, cowboy. I found you."

Leo swung his head around and looked up at him. "Mr. Kingston!" The boy wiped his face. "I wasn't crying." The little dog licked away his tears.

"It's okay. I'm crying because I'm so happy I found you. Nothing wrong with crying, but we need to take a deep breath so we can think." Leo was so close, but with the unstable ground the whole area could collapse.

There was a raging river somewhere below them. He needed ropes, pulleys and a harness. But there was no way he could leave Leo.

"If I let Little Momma stand on my hands, can you get her?" the boy asked.

"I can try. We have to be very careful. We don't want to fall any deeper."

Leo stood, pressing himself against the muddy wall, and reached up with the tiny dog in his hands. When he was fully extended, the dog jumped up and Kingston caught her. "That was very brave, Leo."

"She's safe. How are you getting me out?"

He swallowed hard. There was no way he'd cry right now. Leo had so much faith in him. "I need to find a way to make a harness."

Little Momma started barking, then ran below the rock.

"Kingston?" It was his mother.

"Kingston!" And Naomi. "I hear a dog. Kingston, is that you? Leo?"

"It's Little Momma!" Letti yelled.

"We're behind a huge boulder that slid down the hill," he told them.

"Is Leo okay?" They were running toward them.

"Careful. The ground is unstable."

"I'll go up higher and call Abigail." Letti ran past them.

Naomi fell to her knees behind Kingston and put a hand on his ankle. "Hey, Leo. Looks like you found a cave."

"I did. But I don't want to stay in it right now."

"That's smart. We have to be very careful with caves." Concern flooded her eyes. "That sounds like it has a river."

"It's below Leo. He's on a ledge."

His mother slid her way back to them. "Abigail and her brothers are on their way. They called 911."

"Will I get to ride in an ambulance?" The boy sounded too excited at the possibility.

"Are you hurt? Did you hit your head or black out?" Kingston asked.

"I don't think so. I'm wet and muddy. I'm better now. I know you won't let me fall."

Kingston stopped breathing. Leo was right. He would do anything to keep Leo and Abigail safe, to keep them in his world.

Even if it meant moving his world to theirs. He loved Abigail and her son. But would that be enough for her to trust him?

Abigail wrapped her arms around her middle, trying to stop her hands from shaking. Her baby was trapped in a cavern. The rain had stopped, but it was getting dark.

Kingston was the closest to Leo. He was flat on his stomach, just inches from the opening. Naomi had grown concerned when Gloria told them Kingston had started following a trail on the north side of the barn. She and

Letti went out that direction. Her brothers had ridden on the path between the two ranch houses and had not seen a hint of Leo.

Now, Isaac and Lucas held up the floodlights Cyrus had brought. Not sure what they were dealing with, Joaquin—who knew the land better than anyone—made them move fifty yards below the rock and gaping hole. "Apparently, Kingston has been lying in the mud since he found Leo. None of us would have ever looked here."

Her brother's always-stoic voice was full of appreciation.

Her son had yelled to her that he was alright and Kingston was going to get him out.

Joaquin and Cyrus encouraged Kingston and Leo as they eased in closer and tossed a rope and harness to Kingston. They had anchored it on three giant live oak trees.

The three men worked together as if they had done this a million times. Any trace of hostility and resentment vanished.

She stopped breathing as Kingston lowered the harness to Leo and talked him through putting it on. Letti wrapped her arm around her. Naomi did the same. "Would it help if we prayed while they get your son out?"

Abigail nodded. Growing up with all men, she had missed her mother and grandmother in her life. Naomi and Letti filled a hole in her heart she hadn't even known she had.

Kingston's childhood had been lonely, but today his two mothers had followed him so he wouldn't be alone. When he had really needed them, they had come to his rescue and were now surrounding her in motherly love and support too.

And her brothers trusted Kingston to get Leo out. In this moment, they were all family.

It didn't take long to pull Leo up and he ran straight for

her. Falling to her knees, she closed her eyes and pulled him against her chest. His small frame, his heartbeat—she never wanted to let him go.

Something wiggled between them, and a muffled meow came from inside his raincoat. She looked down. With a huge grin, her son opened the top of the yellow raincoat, and a black-and-white kitten popped its head out, as wet and muddy as her son. "What's this?"

"Stormy. It ran across the pasture, and it was so little and scared I wanted to rescue it. I didn't want it to be lost in the rain."

"You ran after it without waiting for an adult."

"I'm sorry, Momma."

She pulled him to her again and pressed her cheek to his mud-matted hair. "I was so scared. What if Kingston hadn't found your footprints, or…" She pressed her lips closed. He was too young to understand the fears she would be dealing with for a while.

"But Mr. Kingston found us. He stayed with us until his mom found him. Then you found us and my tios brought the rope."

"Yes, they did." Her brothers were getting a big, hearty dinner.

Cyrus helped Kingston up and patted him on the back. "Great work. If you ever need anything, you call me."

Lucas and Isaac had taken the floodlights closer. Joaquin made a noise of utter awe. She turned as he went down and dropped his head into the hole. Standing over him, Lucas whistled. "That's got to be a forty-foot drop."

Her stomach twisted and she pulled Leo closer. "Careful! Don't get so close."

Cyrus joined them on the edge. "It's not just a hole in the ground. We have a huge cavern under our ranch." He scanned the hole from left to right. "I don't see an end to it either way."

Isaac went to the rock and lowered himself to see inside.

"Isaac! Get out of there." Abigail's still-frantic heart couldn't take it. Yelling at them felt good. "The ground is saturated. I'm not letting Kingston risk himself to save y'all."

Her twin looked at her, his eyes wide. "Speleothems! There are five-foot stalactites and stalagmites. There's a column from floor to ceiling. For calcium to create those formations, it has to be at least 500,000 years old. Probably lots older."

Isaac looked as if he was about to go into the cave. "Isaac, don't you dare! Cyrus, get him."

"It's okay, Abigail. I've got him."

At one point in his life, Isaac was obsessed with dinosaurs and fossils. He had had a huge collection of rocks, all carefully sorted and labeled. "I see bones," he said with too much excitement.

While her brothers marveled at the discovery, she was shaking. Leo had come so close to being lost to her forever. Maybe they weren't going to get dinner.

Kingston walked toward her. Mud was caked in his hair and covered him from head to toe. He took out a white cloth and offered it to her. "I thought you might want to get some of the mud off him. Dry him up a bit."

It was a T-shirt. It had to be one he'd worn under his long-sleeve button-up. She felt frozen, unable to move. The shaking was out of control.

He frowned. "Abigail? What's wrong?"

Licking her lips, she shook her head. "You saved him. We would have never…" Her gaze cut to the hillside where her brothers and his moms stared down the hole. A forty-foot drop, covered by a fallen tree.

His arms came around her and Leo. His tall frame surrounded them, holding her together. She couldn't lose it in front of Leo, not completely. It would scare him.

With Kingston's arms around them, she was able to breathe. The three of them clung to each other.

"I'm always going to be here for you. Always." His voice was guttural as his lips moved close to her ear. "I love you."

Closing her eyes, she pulled Leo closer with one arm and wrapped another around Kingston. "It was traumatic to find him but not have help. Don't say—"

"I've loved you for a while, but today I realized I loved you enough to want to stay in your world for as long as you'll let me. Being on solid ground with you and Leo safely in my arms is all I need. I don't want to lose it."

Tilting her head, she made eye contact with him. "What about Dallas and Axel?"

"I want to train and breed horses." He gave her a lopsided grin. "A ranch can be a good place for that. It doesn't have to be racehorses. Maybe Axel will join me here or not. But I'm staying."

"You're staying on the ranch forever?" Leo asked. Having had enough of the hugging, he wiggled free. "Please say yes. Stormy needs a place to stay. She likes Little Momma now and Baby can be her best friend. Tito won't let me keep a cat."

Kingston was smiling at her son, love in his eyes. With her arm still around him, she gave him a quick kiss, not able to hold back her feelings. They were all covered in mud, and she didn't care. "I love you too," she whispered.

The words were out and there was no pretending anymore. For a long moment, they just stayed in each other's gaze. She loved this man so much.

But he was on an adrenaline high. Were his words real?

He bent lower until they were eye to eye. "I will love you tomorrow and the day after and all the days after that. Come rain or shine, my heart is yours. The words are new, but the feeling isn't."

She absorbed the words into her bones.

He turned to the group on the hill. "We're cold, wet and muddy. Y'all can explore the new cave. I'm taking Abigail and Leo home." *Home*. His hand slid down to hers and entwined their fingers. He held out his other hand to Leo and he took it.

"Kingston!" Lucas yelled. They all stiffened. "Thank you. For the record, I think you'd make a good DeLeon."

With a laugh, Kingston pulled Abigail in the direction of the path down the hill. "I'm not sure how to deal with your brothers not hating me."

"Soon they'll love you like I do." She stopped him and pointed to the cedar break. "I have the Gator over there. Your moms are in Bumble Bee."

He grinned. "My moms. I like that."

The clouds broke and opened the sky for the last rays of the sun to highlight his face. She wanted to skip to the UTV. Her world had just shifted in the best possible way.

She loved Kingston Zayas, and he loved her.

Epilogue

$\sim$

Once the area was dry, they discovered the cavern went on for over a mile. The opening and the largest room were under the DeLeon ranch, but the largest percentage stretched under Tres Amigos. So, both families owned a part of the cavern.

Kingston sighed. The families were meeting for the fourth time in one of the newly renovated rooms in the old hacienda. Nail guns, drills and electric saws could still be heard across the courtyard, but no one at the table was bothered by it.

They were too busy arguing. Except Isaac. He seemed very agitated.

Kingston's confidence dipped a little. If Abigail's twin lost focus, his whole plan would fall apart.

Isaac stood. "Until we call experts to look at the scientific and historical impact of the cavern, we should not be discussing this."

Rigo snorted. "I ain't letting the government or those academia people on my land. They'll just start telling me what I can and can't do."

"I think Isaac has a good point. We don't want to destroy what took more than half a million years to develop." Kingston did happen to agree with Isaac. Maybe that would help him refocus.

The next-to-youngest DeLeon sibling nodded to him then walked out of the room. Abigail's gaze followed her twin.

No. No. Don't go after him. Kingston stretched his leg under the table and tapped her foot. She looked at him with a tilt of her head. He pointed his chin to the rest of their family, hoping to redirect her attention.

Naomi crossed her arms. "Yes. We should have experts look at the cave. But we should make plans to open it to the public. It can be a huge revenue maker. We could even host weddings and events in the main chamber."

Cyrus leaned over the table and glared at her. "That would cost too much money, and we don't want strangers walking all over our land. This is a working cattle ranch. Some people at this table respect traditions."

Kingston raised his brows at Abigail. She rolled her eyes and grinned at him.

"I say we cover the hole up and forget it's there. It's nothing but trouble," her grandfather huffed.

They were open and honest in their arguments, just like a real family. They were all his family now. All part of his new home.

The night his barn and apartment burned, he'd thought it was the end to a dream. But God had dreamed bigger plans for him, so much better than he would have ever imagined.

Abigail's and his phones chimed but no one at the table other than them noticed. She turned it over and read it. He read his and smiled. *It was on.*

She got up from the table and left the room. He was right behind her. She turned. "Isaac said Leo had something to show me. I hope everything's okay."

"I'm sure it's fine. I got the text too." Well, not the exact same one. Suddenly, caterpillars were crawling in his gut. What if it didn't work out or she wasn't on the same page?

They passed the office and went down the path they had

followed that first night they met. "Do you know what's going on?"

He just shrugged and reminded himself to breathe.

As they approached the gate between the two ranches, she stopped. "What is this?"

Isaac saw them and waved, then left toward the DeLeon house. Under the giant oak strung with lights, Leo wiggled, holding a basket. Dakota and Fuego stood at the fence.

When they got closer, Little Momma rushed out to greet them. Leo had both kittens. A thick blanket was spread over the ground and a picnic basket sat in the middle.

"Surprise, Momma!"

"This is a surprise, but it's not my birthday." She glanced at him. "Did you plan this?"

"I did." His mouth went dry. "I have a business proposition I would like to discuss."

She raised her brow and dropped her chin. "A business proposition?"

"Yes. Fuego has turned into an outstanding ranch horse. Axel ran into a guy that takes offtrack racehorses and trains them for ranch work. He says thoroughbreds are fast, agile and smart. They can't do the heavy lifting quarter horses do, but they can outwork them in long distance. I think we saw that when you rode Fuego out last week. He really loved the work."

Her eyes searched his, a hint of confusion in them. She tilted her head and studied him. "I agree, but why are we out here?"

He was messing this up. Eyes to the sky, he blew out a puff of air and regrouped his thoughts.

"I'm giving you Fuego as a gift." He pointed to the stallion.

She turned and looked, then gasped. "The saddle. It's the one from Carter's that I loved."

"It's yours, and so is Fuego." His insides were a mess.

She went to the horse and talked to him, rubbing under his jaw just the way he liked. Then she moved to his side and mounted. "He's mine? Are you sure? This is too much, Kingston."

"Mr. Kingston! You're forgetting the best part!" Leo was jumping, then sat down. "Sorry. I promised not to run or yell. I'm just so excited and Mr. Kingston's not doing it right."

He laughed. "Thanks for redirecting me, Leo."

Standing next to her, he put a hand on her leg and looked up. "There's something in the saddlebag." She twisted and pulled a small pouch out.

Her jaw dropped when she saw the ring.

She went still, no reaction. Had he had gotten it wrong?

"I asked Leo first. I wanted it to be okay with him if I became your husband and his father. He said yes. I asked Isaac and I told my moms. They're excited to call you Daughter, officially. They said you were already the daughter of their hearts. You're my forever home, Abigail DeLeon. Will you marry me?"

He was out of breath. She just held the ring and stared at it. Tears were welling up in her eyes.

"Oh no. Sweetheart, I didn't mean to make you cry." He covered her hands with his.

She looked down at him. "I made a promise to not marry again until Leo was older."

The blood left his body. He wanted to say something, anything to prove to her she could trust him. But the words lodged in his throat.

Her gaze moved to Leo, then to him. "But then God brought you into my life and everything changed."

"Mom! Say yes. Please. We love Mr. Kingston and he loves us."

She nodded. "I know. That's why I'm changing my plan. Kingston Zayas, let's make a home together."

He took the ring and slipped it in place, both of their hands shaking. Swinging her leg over, she put her hands on his shoulders and her boots on the ground.

"Yes. She said yes." Leo danced around.

They laughed. "You didn't mention asking my grand-father for permission."

"Oh no. I respect your grandfather, but he still kind of scares me. Did you know they invited me to help with moving the cattle across the river? That's good, right?"

"From an old Texas rancher that's the best stamp of approval." She grinned. "Ask for forgiveness instead of permission?"

"Yep. That was my thought. Naomi and Letti are giving us Treetop Cabin. We can add on to it. I think it would be a perfect home."

"I agree. But then again, if I'm with you, I'd be happy making the bunkhouse our home."

Home. The dream he had thought forever out of his reach was now in his arms. And he would hold her close for the rest of his life.

* * * * *

If you liked this story from Jolene Navarro,
check out her previous Love Inspired books:

The Texan's Journey Home
The Reluctant Rancher
Bound by a Secret

Available now from Love Inspired!

Find more great reads at www.LoveInspired.com.

Dear Reader,

Thank you for joining me as I return home to the Texas Hill Country to kick off this new series, The Ranchers of Rio Bella. The DeLeons have been knocking on my door for a while. With Kingston and Abigail, I wanted to explore the idea that sometimes we work hard for something we want, and when it's lost or never materializes, we feel lost. But what if it wasn't God's plan for us? What if we were meant to be doing something else? I loved bringing these two to their HEA.

I live a few miles from Cave Without A Name and have wanted to use a cave for years. The DeLeon and Zayas families were perfect to find it. I hope you enjoyed reading their story as much as I enjoyed discovering it. I'm excited to announce that Joaquin and his service dogs will be out in time for Christmas.

I can be found at jolenenavarroauthor@gmail.com and on Facebook.